Vampire

Also From Rebecca Zanetti

DARK PROTECTORS
Fated
Claimed
Tempted novella
Hunted
Consumed
Provoked
Twisted novella
Shadowed
Tamed novella
Marked
Teased novella
Tricked novella
Tangled novella
Talen novella
Vampire's Faith
Demon's Mercy
Alpha's Promise
Hero's Haven
Guardian's Grace
Immortal's Honor
Garrett's Destiny

THE ANNA ALBERTINI FILES
Disorderly Conduct
Bailed Out
Adverse Possession
Holiday Rescue Novella
Santa's Subpoena

DEEP OPS
Hidden
Taken novella
Fallen
Shaken novella
Broken

Vampire

A Dark Protectors/Rebels Novella

By Rebecca Zanetti

1001 DARK NIGHTS
PRESS

Vampire
A Dark Protectors/Rebels Novella
By Rebecca Zanetti

Copyright 2021 Rebecca Zanetti
ISBN: 978-1-951812-39-3

Foreword: Copyright 2014 M. J. Rose

Published by 1001 Dark Nights Press, an imprint of Evil Eye Concepts, Incorporated

Dedication

This one is for the entire Evil Eye/1001 Dark Nights crew. I love you all!

Sign up for the 1001 Dark Nights Newsletter
and be entered to win a Tiffany Key necklace.

There's a contest every month!

Go to www.1001DarkNights.com to subscribe.

As a bonus, all subscribers can download
FIVE FREE exclusive books!

Acknowledgments from the Author

A huge thank you to Liz Berry, MJ Rose, and Jillian Stein for banding together this amazing group of authors who have become such good friends.

Thanks also to the entire 1001 Dark Night team: Kimberly Guidroz, Kasi Alexander, Asha Hossain, and Jenn Watson from Social Butterfly. Also thanks to Anissa Beatty and the entire FB Rebecca's Rebels Street Team for the support!

Finally, a huge thank you to my family, Big Tone, Gabe, and Karlina for the support and laughs. I love you three.

One Thousand and One Dark Nights

Once upon a time, in the future…

*I was a student fascinated with stories and learning.
I studied philosophy, poetry, history, the occult, and
the art and science of love and magic. I had a vast
library at my father's home and collected thousands
of volumes of fantastic tales.*

*I learned all about ancient races and bygone
times. About myths and legends and dreams of all
people through the millennium. And the more I read
the stronger my imagination grew until I discovered
that I was able to travel into the stories... to actually
become part of them.*

*I wish I could say that I listened to my teacher
and respected my gift, as I ought to have. If I had, I
would not be telling you this tale now.
But I was foolhardy and confused, showing off
with bravery.*

*One afternoon, curious about the myth of the
Arabian Nights, I traveled back to ancient Persia to
see for myself if it was true that every day Shahryar
(Persian: شهریار, "king") married a new virgin, and then
sent yesterday's wife to be beheaded. It was written
and I had read, that by the time he met Scheherazade,
the vizier's daughter, he'd killed one thousand
women.*

*Something went wrong with my efforts. I arrived
in the midst of the story and somehow exchanged
places with Scheherazade – a phenomena that had
never occurred before and that still to this day, I
cannot explain.*

*Now I am trapped in that ancient past. I have
taken on Scheherazade's life and the only way I can
protect myself and stay alive is to do what she did to
protect herself and stay alive.*

*Every night the King calls for me and listens as I spin tales.
And when the evening ends and dawn breaks, I stop at a
point that leaves him breathless and yearning for more.
And so the King spares my life for one more day, so that
he might hear the rest of my dark tale.*

*As soon as I finish a story... I begin a new
one... like the one that you, dear reader, have before
you now.*

Chapter 1

A pristine bouquet of white roses lay gently across the *Happy Autumn* welcome mat on her weathered front porch. Mariana froze mere feet away, grocery bags in her hands, as the breeze lightly lifted a couple of petals.

He'd found her.

She dropped the bags and dug her gun out of her purse, swinging her gaze around the peaceful neighborhood. Nothing but lively trees bursting with red, orange, and yellow leaves met her gaze as the clouds rolled in above. The houses were spaced a couple of acres apart, and from what she could see, most folks were still at work for the day. As usual, the traffic on the country road was non-existent.

Even so, she side-stepped carefully, gun pointed at the ground, up the stairs and to her door. It was locked. Good.

Entering the cottage, she locked the door behind her and swept the one-story, two-bedroom home. Even though she'd practiced for this, she still held her breath before looking under the beds and behind the shower curtains.

Nothing. She was alone.

Thunder rolled outside, promising a good storm.

She sagged against the wall and let her arm drop. Okay. She was all right. So much for statistics. Usually a stalker gave up and found somebody else to harass when his victim moved across the country. Not this time. She ran for the closet in her bedroom and whipped the doors open to reveal the camera system and punched up the video. Blank. They'd been wiped clean. Her ears started to heat, and she shrugged out of her jacket. She fumbled for her phone in her back pocket and dialed a direct line in the Dallas Police Department.

"Cooley," came a distracted voice.

"Hi, Laura. It's Mariana." She slid down the wall to sit on the polished wooden floor.

Silence erupted across the line. "M? What the hell? Why are you calling? We decided—"

"He found me. White roses across my front porch," Mariana said wearily.

Papers rustled. "Shit. How did he find you? Have you kept in touch with anybody?" Laura's voice lowered.

"No. I stuck to the plan." Most of the plan had been over the top, as far as Mariana had thought. Turned out she was wrong. "I only have a burner phone, and I change it every month. Haven't talked to a soul from Texas, haven't used credit cards, and I've stayed off the Internet. He's better than we thought." Her stomach cramped.

"Crap," Laura muttered. "I've continued working the case, but I have nothing. No clue who this guy is, still. If it even is a guy. If I can't find him, how did he find you? I don't even know where you are."

"Indiana," Mariana said quietly. "Nice town. You should come visit." While her knees were trembling, it was still nice to be talking to her best friend again. "We were wrong that he'd move on to somebody else."

"No kidding," Laura said. "Tell me you caught him on camera. Tell me you installed cameras first thing."

Mariana set her head back and shut her eyes, trying not to vomit. "I installed cameras, and I did not catch him. He found them and wiped them clean. I bought the best I could afford." Which hadn't been much, unfortunately. She opened her eyes and laid the gun on her thigh. "What now?"

"Well, you could come home," Laura said. "If he found you, I'd much rather you were here with me. You can have my spare bedroom."

Mariana stared at the floor she'd lovingly restored after hours and on weekends. She'd made this home hers. "No, but thanks. I obviously can't run from this guy, because he'll keep finding me. I love this small town, and I've gotten some good clients even without using my credentials. Since he's found me, I can register and get licensed with the state and really get back to work."

"You are a great shrink," Laura agreed. "I don't have any time off, or I'd head your way and help you. For now, how about I reach out to the local authorities and collaborate?"

Mariana let a small laugh escape. "Give it two weeks, would you? The current sheriff is a dumbass, but the guy running for the position is excellent. I'm actually helping with the campaign." It probably wouldn't hurt to let Evan in on her problems, since he'd been a good cop before being fired. Especially since he'd seemed so much healthier the last couple of months than when she'd arrived in town. For a bit, she'd been afraid he was really ill. Guess not. He would make a great sheriff, if he won.

"If the horse you're backing doesn't win, you have to promise me you'll come home. In fact, why don't you head this way for the next couple of weeks?" Laura asked.

Mariana shook her head. "This guy will find me again, and I'm done running." Although she wasn't a moron and would definitely ask Evan for help.

Laura hummed quietly. "I don't suppose you'd hire a bodyguard?"

Now Mariana barked out a full laugh. "With what? My sparkling eyes and great sense of humor? It took everything I had to repair this place and get it up to snuff. Aunt Florence let it go a little bit."

"There had to have been a connection we missed between you and Florence that made you traceable," Laura mused.

"Nope. Florence was my grandma's best friend, and I called her Aunt Florence, but we weren't related in any way. She lived all over the world and just moved here a few years ago, and while we somewhat kept in touch, it wasn't much. I was shocked she left me the house after she died." The woman had sent Mariana the documents in the mail right before dying. Mariana eyed the gun on her leg. "I haven't recorded the quitclaim deed, so there's no public record that I own the property. I can't be traced to this home, so that's not how he found me."

Laura sighed. "All right. I take it you also haven't changed your driver's license or anything else?"

"Nope," Mariana said, her senses heightened as she listened for any sounds outside that shouldn't be there. "I need to go and make sure the house is locked up tight." Although she'd just checked. "I'll call you first thing tomorrow, and maybe we can figure out a game plan." Since the guy wouldn't give up, she had no choice but to find him.

"Promise you'll call your friends—especially the ex-cop guy who's about to be the sheriff," Laura said.

"Definitely. Bye." Mariana ended the conversation and quickly dialed Evan to leave a message for him to call her back as soon as possible. Then she stood, slipped her phone into her pocket and her gun into her waistband, and double-checked the locks on all windows and the two doors. Okay. She was secure. Her heart still beat too fast and her head ached, but for now, she was safe.

The kitchen door to the garage burst open with a loud clatter and bounced against the fridge.

She screamed and reached for her gun, but it was too late. A hood was slammed on her head, and a man who felt to be at least twice her size turned and carried her into the garage and out the side door to a quietly running vehicle she hadn't seen beyond the thicket of trees. She blinked but only saw darkness. She hadn't even seen his face.

* * * *

Raine Maxwell was going to kill somebody. At the moment, with a hood over his head, he wasn't sure who. Even though he was just regaining consciousness, he already had an idea, though. "Whoever darted me is going to pay. Take the hood off. Now," he growled. His hands were tied behind his back, and he sat on a cold dirt floor. As the sedative coursed through his system, his strength began to return. The wind whispered her secrets through slats of wood at his shoulders, and if he pushed hard enough, he could go right through to the rainy night outside. Yet he remained still. "Last chance."

Then he paused and listened. Nothing but wind.

He sniffed. Dirt, rain, and hay. He was alone? Somebody had gone to the trouble to knock him out, bring him to some barn, and then leave his ass? Oh, he didn't think so. His left hand trembled—a condition he was becoming accustomed to.

What had awoken him? An engine, still running outside, caught his attention.

Then a door opened, and heavy footsteps pounded across the dirt. Something was hefted to the floor and then the footsteps rapidly escaped. An engine revved up outside and then a vehicle with a loud engine sped away.

What was happening? Raine reared up and paused as a scent hit him. A powerful one of female, honey, and pears. Everything inside him settled and then supercharged. "Mariana?" he whispered.

She screamed, high and loud.

He jumped to his feet and lowered his head, shaking wildly until the hood flew off. His hands remained bound, and he pivoted to take in the entire barn. It was empty except for the female sitting across from him, her hands bound in back of her and a hood covering her head. A lit lantern perched on a bale of hay to her right. "You're okay." He took a deep breath and jerked on his restraints, ripping them open as he regained his strength. He strode to her and crouched down, taking off her hood.

She shrank away and knocked her head against the worn siding. "Get away from me."

He remained in place, his gaze searching. Power and strength flowed through him just from being near her for a few minutes. "Did they hurt you?"

She stared at him and then recognition lightened her stunning brown eyes. "Raine?" she croaked.

His lungs compressed and then heated with lava. "Yeah." Whoever had done this to her would cry in pain. "Talk to me. Are you hurt?" He tried to keep his voice gentle, but the tenor lowered to gritty and hoarse.

She just stared. Her dark hair was wild around her heart-shaped face, but he couldn't see any bruises on her.

"Let's get these off you." He angled to the side and gently pulled her forward so he could see her restraints. Simple ties. He broke them with one finger. Yeah. Her nearness already brought some of his strength back to him. The legends about his family were true.

The second her hands were free, she twirled away from him and leaped to her feet, backing away. "I can't believe it's you. All of this time." Her voice shook as she reached in her waistband and came away empty.

He scratched his whiskered chin. "What's me?"

She gulped in air, and her gaze caught on one of the silver restraints still hanging from his wrist. Then she swung her focus to where his hood lay near where he'd sat. "Oh, God. This is my fault. He got you, too?"

Raine paused and lowered his chin to better see her eyes. Was she concussed? How the hell was he going to explain this to her? "I was knocked out and just came to as you were brought in. I—"

"I'm so sorry." She rushed for him and grabbed his hands. "This is my fault. But why you? Were you coming to my place? I don't understand." She released him and looked around. "We have to get out of here. How did you break your cuffs? They look solid. Even more than my ties had."

The woman's thoughts bounced around faster than his fury. He had to make her understand that he hadn't asked for this clusterfuck. "Mariana—"

"Oh." She slapped her hand over her mouth and then removed it. "You were bringing back that dish you borrowed right before you disappeared from town." She shook her head. "Right? That's the only way he could've seen you." She swallowed rapidly. "Where did you go, anyway?"

Away from her. As far away from her as he could get—and he'd kept the dish like a moron just so he could remember her. It was plain and slightly pink, and she'd brought cookies on it to the first fundraiser for Evan Holden, who was running for sheriff. Raine had promised to return it to her, and then he'd split town. Fast. "I went home to Montana and had just gotten back to town this morning. I was on my way to your place when I was hit with a bunch of darts." He hadn't been able to stay away any longer, and look what that had gotten him. Yet it felt damn good to regain some of his strength. Because of her.

Her gaze darted around, and fear rolled off her. "He must've taken you before I even got home. I'm so sorry about this."

"He?" Raine tried to get his brain to full power. "No one man could've taken me out, sweetheart." Darts or not. He had a bad suspicion and hustled to the door to look out at the darkness. "Where are we?"

"If you were darted, one small child could've knocked you out," she countered, her voice trembling. "Although it'd take a strong man, maybe two, to get you into the trunk of a car. He didn't sedate me but did put me in the trunk of a car, and it had to be at least a two or three hour drive," she said, moving to his side to look out at the slashing rain and dark night. "We have to get out of here."

Wait a minute. He'd been out for hours after being sedated? What had been in those darts? Had he become that weak already without her? Oh, he was going to kill somebody. "Did they hurt you?" he growled.

"Not yet." She manacled her nails into his forearm. "This is my fault. The guy has been stalking me forever, and he finally got me. I'm not sure where he is right now, but we have to run." Thunder blasted high and loud, and she jumped but set her chin. "We have to go now, Raine."

Wait a minute. Perhaps his brothers hadn't just forced his hand with Mariana. Was there an enemy out there? A real stalker?

Chapter 2

Mariana watched the wind blow the slashing rain sideways toward more darkness. She could make out a muddy road with a thick forest on one side and what looked like weeds on the other that extended far into the abyss. It must've been a field at some time. She shivered. "If we stay to the trees, we'll have some shelter."

Raine remained silent at her side.

She could almost feel his mind working, and the tension pouring from him was actually speeding up her heart rate even faster, if that was possible. At the moment, she could barely breathe. She'd been taken, gotten him kidnapped, and they were now abandoned in this weird barn.

For now.

Her breath burst out. "They'll be coming back. Or he will." She ran through the issues even as her legs trembled with the need to escape into the storm. "He must've had somebody else kidnap us?" What did that mean? Did the guy want an alibi if she was taken? Or was he unable to kidnap somebody like Raine? If so, did that mean he was smaller than Raine? Or did it mean that her stalker was a woman? Her gut had always felt it was a man, but maybe she was wrong. "We have to go, Raine." Yet she stayed in place. Was there more danger in the storm or in the barn? The barn. The kidnappers could return with weapons. They surely hadn't expected Raine to be able to get out of his cuffs.

"We have to wait out the storm, darlin'." Raine put one broad hand on the door as if to shut it.

She whirled on him, thankful to have a place to focus. "You don't understand."

"Yeah. We're gonna discuss that." He looked down at her, formidable now that the drugs had obviously exited his system.

Before she'd met him, months ago, she hadn't believed in love at first sight. Or even lust at first sight. But without knowing it, without having a clue that she dreamed about him every night, he'd taught her that it existed.

The unexplainable.

Oh, she wanted him, but it went deeper than that. She didn't understand why, and there was no doubt the attraction was one-sided, but she'd always dream about him. It just was. For now, she had to save his life.

She grabbed his arm. He wasn't understanding the danger here. "Listen to me. Please." She looked way up to his hard cut face. From the first day, she'd found him to be unreal. His eyes glittered a fierce green against his darker complexion. His bone structure was sharply angled, his eyebrows naturally arched, and his jawline sliced with expert precision. He had jet-black hair that was thick and wavy, and his body was muscled and graceful. He was beautiful in a wild and raw way—too rough to be a model but more stunning than any man she'd ever seen.

He slipped out of his battered leather jacket and set it around her shoulders. "Put your arms in."

She didn't have the energy to argue and was freezing, so she did as he'd ordered. His intriguing scent of male with a hint of coffee beans surrounded her. She really did imagine that scent in her dreams. "He's going to show up. We have to run."

Raine arched one very dark eyebrow. "I hope he comes back. Or they do. I'm not sedated right now, and you're safe. Take a deep breath before you hyperventilate."

Her body flushed cold and then very warm. Oh, he stood to about six and a half feet tall, was muscled, and moved like he could fight. Even so, this kidnapping was obviously planned out, and right now, Raine didn't have a weapon on him. "You're a badass, I admit. But even you can't outrun a bullet." She wouldn't feel guilty about the relief filtering through her that she wasn't alone here. "Let's run for the trees."

"No." He kept the door open but pulled her back. "I can see if anybody comes down that road, and if they do, they're going to regret it. For now, tell me what's going on."

There was a difference between being brave and being an egotistical moron, and Mariana had to get him to see reason. While Raine was tough, the kidnapper had both sedatives and probably weapons, and getting to safety was more important than fighting right now. So she did the only thing she could by ducking her head, bunching her legs, and running full-on into the rain.

Lightning zigged on the field, lighting the entire world and blowing the harsh smell of ozone at her. She screamed and ran faster over the muddy ground, hunching over and beating toward the forest. Rain poured over her, instantly soaking her hair to her head. She blinked water out of her eyes.

Her escape must've surprised Raine, because it took him a moment to catch up with her. When he did, it wasn't to help her into the trees.

He snatched her up in a move so fast she got dizzy and had to close her eyes. He swung them around and ran back into the barn, setting her roughly on a bale of old and prickly hay. "What the holy fuck are you doing?" His eyes blazed an impossible green in his brutal face.

She kicked his shin and tried to jump to her feet.

He planted one solid hand over her entire shoulder and kept her in place. "Knock it off," he growled.

She stiffened and sucked in several panicked breaths. "What are you doing?"

His jaw firmed, and he just stared at her. When he spoke, he sounded like he'd swallowed sharp stones. "You were the tallest thing away from the forest, and there's lightning out there. We're not going anywhere until this storm abates. Period."

She swallowed. "We have to run. The guy has a plan, Raine."

"Good. So do I." He loomed over her, looking more dangerous than any stalker could ever be.

"What's that?" she snapped, searching for her temper and thankfully finding it.

He leaned toward her, masculine and intense. "We wait out the storm. If it lets up, we walk to the nearest town. If the kidnapper shows up, I rip off his head. That's the plan."

* * * *

Raine's temper was a slow burn, and at the moment, the wick was ignited. He released the female and took a step back to give her some breathing room. If her chest panted any faster, she'd go into a full-on panic attack, and he needed to know what he was dealing with here. Maybe the kidnapping hadn't been focused on him. In fact, it was looking less likely at the moment. "Okay. Tell me what's going on." He tried to keep his tone gentle, but as a demon-vampire hybrid, his voice would always be hoarse.

She wiped rain off her pretty face and pulled her wet hair out of his jacket. "Fine, but if he shows up, I'm running. You're being a moron."

Good. Her spunk was back. "I promise I can handle anything coming our way." Now that he knew something or somebody was coming their way. He'd been embarrassingly unprepared earlier because his mind had been filled with her. The one woman he should stay the hell away from. Plus, his strength had waned being away from her for weeks. "Who do you think kidnapped us?" God, it was embarrassing to even admit he'd lowered his guard enough to *be* kidnapped.

Her eyes were dark pools of fear and anger. "I don't know who he is. I'm assuming it's a man, because statistically most stalkers are male, but I don't even know that fact for sure. Although my gut tells me it is a man, for some reason."

Okay. "Is this a recent event?" Who in their small town would be stalking her?

She huddled deeper into his jacket, looking small and defenseless. "No. It started in Dallas, which is one of the reasons I moved to Indiana, besides my adopted aunt leaving me her cottage."

"What started?" He kept his voice as calm as possible under the circumstances.

She took a deep breath and slowly exhaled. "Greeting cards were sent to my office, then white roses, and then more elaborate gifts, including a diamond bracelet. Then phone calls with hang-ups, and the police eventually tracked those all down to burner phones."

"What were the messages?" he asked.

She paled and then shrugged. "They were mostly positive about love and the future and destiny. At least at first. The tone of the notes turned darker and angrier as time went on, because whatever I was supposed to do, in this psycho's fantasy, I wasn't doing. Although there's no way to know what I was supposed to do."

Yeah, sounded like a nut job. A human one. So this might not have anything to do with Raine or his family, although he wasn't taking that suspicion off the table as of yet. "Did the police have any suspects?"

She shook her head. "No. We went through all of my clients, friends, and acquaintances, and nobody stood out. It's entirely possible I don't know this person at all, and we just had some chance encounter they made into much more. I've wracked my brain but haven't come up with anything." Her mouth turned down, and the sense of fear from her increased.

"I'm not going to let anything happen to you," he said quietly, meaning every word.

A small, rueful smile tilted her peach-colored lips. "That's sweet, but I already got you drugged and kidnapped."

Man, she was cute. Gorgeous, really. Her eyes were the color of dark and genuine topaz rocks, her hair black, and her bone structure royal. "He caught me off guard, sweetheart. Now I know he's out there." Life would be easier if he could just tell her he was immortal, but that would put her into even more danger, considering secrecy was key for his people. Creating a war between humans and everyone else would be a disaster, and since he wasn't going to bring her into his world, he had to keep his secrets. "You can trust me."

She stood, and this time he let her. "You were my patient, and I should be handling this."

The woman barely came to his shoulder. Humor lightened the stress attacking him for the briefest of moments. "I was never your patient, and you know it. I attended your anger management group because of a job and not because I have anger issues." They'd met in an anger-management group that the woman still had no idea was more full of immortal intrigue than true anger.

She frowned, looking like an angry and rather sexy librarian. "Excuse me?"

He attempted to keep the smile off his face. "Yeah. I was investigating a couple of the other members and had to be there. I don't have anger issues, and if you recall, I didn't really share."

"Who were you investigating?" She tried to put her hands on her hips, but the enormous jacket prevented her movements.

"Noah and his buddy Ivar," Raine admitted. Noah and Ivar were both immortal hybrids, and Ivar was dangerous to the point that Raine thought he might have to kill the guy. It was a good thing he didn't, because he'd ended up friends with Noah Siosal.

Mariana gasped. "You're a detective?"

"Um, no. It's a long story, and I can't go into it with you." Ivar was one of the immortal members of an elite group called the Seven, and as a very distant cousin of Raine's, he knew about the Maxwell family secret, which couldn't go public. In fact, now there seemed to be no doubt that Benny had helped engineer the entire situation to not only help Ivar, but to force Raine into proximity with Mariana in the anger-management group under the guise of having Raine keep an eye on Ivar.

The question was which one of Raine's brothers had gotten Benny involved. Raine had intended to leave Mariana alone after she'd moved from Dallas to Indiana, but Benny and Ivar had changed that—along with help from the Maxwell family.

But Raine could handle his family and keep Mariana safe at the same time. "But it's all good now," Raine added.

"All good?" Her voice rose. "You attended a confidential group under pretense." Her frown only made her more beautiful. "Ivar left very early and yet you stayed. Why?"

Because of her. Because he couldn't stand to be away from her, even though that had to be his path. He wouldn't endanger her, and that was that. "I can't tell you," he murmured. Did her pretty mouth taste like peaches? Man, he had to stop thinking like that.

She socked him right in the gut. Hard.

It was the second time he'd been caught off guard that day. He had to get a grip on himself.

The rain started to lessen outside.

She rubbed her wrist. "That's it. I'm out of here." Without waiting for a response, she marched right to the door.

He sighed. This was going to be more difficult than he'd feared. There was no way he could leave her right now—not until taking out her stalker.

She looked over her shoulder, her gaze haughty. "The rain is letting up. Are you coming?"

He set his stance. "Oh, I wouldn't miss it."

Chapter 3

Mariana tried to sit taller in the chair on the other side of the sheriff's desk. Her hair had dried and frizzed around her head, mud coated her legs, and her hands would not warm up. Raine lounged next to her, irritation carving lines in his face. "Sheriff, thank you for seeing us," she said, trying to keep the edge out of her voice. They'd had to wait a half an hour in the waiting room.

"Sorry to keep you waiting," the sheriff said, not sounding sorry at all. He rubbed a beefy hand through his buzz cut hair before hitching his pants up over his slight beer belly. "I was working on my campaign, considering I have an opponent this time."

Yeah. An opponent Mariana had been helping to campaign. "I see," she said quietly, letting her tone speak volumes.

Raine stretched lazily. "This is a waste of time."

Yeah, she'd had to argue with him about making a police report of their kidnapping, but he'd finally relented. "We need a record about this to create a good case once we find this guy," she reminded him. Again.

The sheriff looked them both over. "All right. You mentioned to the deputy at reception that you were both kidnapped and held at the old, abandoned barn at the McPearson place."

"McPearson place?" Mariana asked.

The sheriff nodded. "Yeah. The elder McPearson died a couple of years ago and left the property to the county, but there's not much to do with it. We do have a 4th of July party out there every year. I'll send a deputy to look around, but it sounds like you were just dumped there."

Mariana rubbed dirt off her pants. "How would kidnappers know about the place?"

"Everyone knows about that place. It's even on the website for the town," the sheriff affirmed.

Great. That didn't help.

The sheriff looked them over. "Were you rolled in the mud?"

What a putz. The guy was in his thirties but had the belligerent tone of an angry teenager. Mariana plastered on her most professional smile. "We had to walk several miles in the rain and mud until a nice farmer picked us up in his old truck. Since it was full, we had to sit in the back, and it started to rain again. We're lucky to be here so early, Sheriff."

The sheriff drew out a notepad. "All right. Start from the beginning."

Mariana cleared her throat and then told the sheriff the entire story, starting with the stalking events in Dallas and watching as he kept diligent notes. When she wound down, he looked up at her, his head tilted.

Then he focused on Raine. "Is this what you corroborate?" he asked.

Raine nodded. "Yep."

"Interesting." The sheriff sat back and placed his hands on his belly. "Let me get this straight. You were drugged, came to in the barn right after Miss Lopez was brought in, strongly shook off your hood, and then magically broke the cuffs binding you?"

Raine didn't so much as twitch. "Yep."

The sheriff swung his sharp gaze to her. "Have you thought this through?"

She blinked, heat swirling through her. "What do you mean?"

The sheriff's smile wasn't kind. "Are you believing this crap? You said that his cuffs were metal. How did he break them after being darted with so much sedative that he was knocked out for at least two, maybe three hours?"

She chewed on her bottom lip, her mind spinning. That was a good point. "I heard his cuffs break." But how did he break silver cuffs? She couldn't even get out of her zip ties, and he'd gotten her right out of them without a knife. She turned toward Raine. "Raine?"

He looked her way, his gaze veiled. "Please. The cuffs were weak."

The sheriff motioned for a couple of deputies in the bullpen. "You know what I think?"

"I don't care," Raine replied lazily, when the tension from him was anything but calm.

Mariana looked back and forth between them, trying to reconcile her brain with her gut. A lot of the evening didn't make sense, but why would

Raine kidnap her?

The door opened, and two deputies walked in.

The sheriff remained in place. "I think you kidnapped Miss Lopez and then pretended to rescue her. It's the only thing that makes sense."

Raine snorted. "It's Dr. Lopez, and I didn't rescue her. She rescued herself and then a farmer older than this building rescued us both and drove us to town. Tell me, Sheriff. If I went to all the trouble to kidnap Mariana, why the hell would I just let her go?"

It was a good question. Mariana slowly turned her attention to the sheriff.

The sheriff stared at Raine. "Well, now. He did rescue you, *Dr.* Lopez, and now you have a shared experience. Has he offered to protect you yet?"

She shifted uneasily on the seat. "No." Well, not really. Raine had said that he wasn't going to let anything happen to her. That was kind of an offer of protection. This didn't make any sense. Raine Maxwell was the hot alpha guy of all time. Even when they'd just walked through the bullpen, the two female officers had sighed. Loudly.

The sheriff scoffed. "I can see your mind working fast. Some of the most prolific serial killers in this world have been good-looking men."

It was true, and it was slightly disconcerting that the lawman had read her so correctly. She turned back to him. Maybe he wasn't as stupid as she'd thought, which made him lazy and bad at his job. "Raine didn't carry me into that barn." She knew his scent, which she wasn't going to admit. Plus, if she'd been over his shoulder from the car to the barn, she would've known it was him. She couldn't explain how.

"So his partner did," the sheriff said. "Who's your partner, Maxwell? Give it up now, and I'll make sure the judge goes lightly on you."

Raine's jaw clenched. "I work alone, buddy. Always have and always will." He turned that glittering green gaze on Mariana. "I didn't kidnap you, and I think you know that. I'm not a game player, and I would never stretch anything out this long. You know that, too."

Everything she knew about him proved that to be true. Although how well did she know him? He'd never really contributed in the group sessions, and she'd only just learned that he came from Montana. Also, he could've kidnapped her before now if he'd wanted. Even so, she had to be smart. "Have you ever been to Dallas?"

"No," he said before turning to the sheriff. "I've had enough of this. Take down the report and then do your job." He stood up and set a hand beneath Mariana's arm to help her up.

The sheriff stood. "Oh. I wasn't clear. You're under arrest for the kidnapping and false imprisonment of Miss Mariana Lopez." He smiled. "Excuse me. Dr. Mariana Lopez."

* * * *

Raine's head was about to blow off his shoulders. His temper had fully spiked, and he calculated how quickly he could decapitate the sheriff and both deputies. Oh, he wouldn't do it, but it eased his anger to at least contemplate the matter. "I have lawyers who will descend on this town like buzzards on a body, Sheriff. You don't have probable cause to arrest me, and if you do, I'll take everything you have." Where the hell was he going to find lawyers around here?

The sheriff paused. "I have enough on you with just the broken cuffs."

Raine forced a smile, acutely aware of the threats in front and behind of Mariana. He had to get her out of there so he could breathe again. "No, you don't. In addition, I have three cousins who work for national news organizations, and I'll have them writing stories about small town corruption and your office within ten minutes. Try me. The campaign for your office will be over before one person goes to the voting booth."

As a bluff, it wasn't his best. By the paling of the sheriff's plump face, he didn't realize that.

The sheriff looked at Mariana, calculation in his eyes. "If you make a report against Mr. Maxwell, I'll have probable cause to keep him for seventy-two hours. If there's even a chance he kidnapped you, don't you want him contained here so you're safe?"

The woman waffled. Based on the indecision on her face, she really didn't know what to believe, and Raine couldn't exactly blame her.

He sighed. "Mariana? I did not kidnap you. Truth be told, I'm fucking embarrassed I was darted and kidnapped with a hood over my head, and if there was a way out of this without telling that truth, I'd find it. You obviously are in danger, and there are questions with no answers that I really need to find."

She frowned, turning more fully toward him. "Like why my stalker would dart you."

"Yeah. More importantly, why were we both dumped in a barn hours from here?" It didn't make any sense that her stalker would want Raine anywhere around. He was the biggest threat, and he should've been taken out while incapacitated.

She rubbed a dot of mud off her chin. "I was thinking about that. If this guy is really nuts, he might want to hurt you in front of me, thinking there was something between us." She chewed on her bottom lip, obviously having been running through scenarios all night in her head. "If he hired somebody to kidnap us, he might've been on the way to the barn, reassured that we were both tied up. Maybe he was slowed down by the storm."

The sheriff slammed his fist on his desk, causing her to jump. "That's ridiculous. Mariana. You have to know how nutty that sounds," he snapped.

A low growl rumbled up Raine's chest, and he ruthlessly swallowed it down. That was the first time the sheriff had referred to her by her first name, and now he sounded concerned instead of condescending. Mariana faltered, looking between them again. Raine ground his palm in his left eye to ward off a looming headache. "I did not engineer this kidnapping."

"I disagree," the sheriff countered.

"Yeah. Want me to arrest him?" the first deputy said.

Mariana partially turned to see him clearly as Raine did the same. "Wait a minute. Johnny?" She whirled to face the sheriff. "You hired your son as a deputy after he failed to attend anger management sessions?"

The man was a moron. Raine shook his head. Johnny was a jerk who'd only attended one session, and he'd hit on Mariana and pissed Raine off within minutes. The kid hadn't come back.

The sheriff stood taller and sucked in his gut. "The judge dismissed all charges, and Deputy Baker here passed all of the requirements. He's a good deputy, but if you want somebody else to arrest Maxwell, that's no problem."

Mariana stood to her full and still small height. "I seriously doubt your abilities now, Sheriff. I will not file any sort of report against Mr. Maxwell, and if you arrest him, I will testify on his behalf that I said so to you. He didn't want to file a report because of the corruption here, and I disagreed. It appears that he was correct and I was wrong."

The sheriff's expression softened. "Mariana. I understand your anger, but please take a moment and think just of yourself. This man is a danger to you, and I can have him off the street long enough for you to figure out what's happening. At the very least, let me do some investigation into his background and find the trail back to Dallas. I really believe he's your stalker. It's the only thing that makes sense."

Johnny leaned forward, his hair cut in a new buzz. "You should listen to my pop. He's a great cop."

Raine could thank the kid for the assist. He should've kept his mouth shut.

"No," Mariana said, eyeing Johnny. "You were arrested several times for beating up your young wife, and then in our group, you were rude and suggestive. It shows poor judgment on your father's behalf that he hired you and gave you a gun." She stiffened. "We're leaving now. Please keep my report on file for the next sheriff." With that zinger, she turned and pushed her way between the deputies and out of the office.

Raine watched her as a very unwelcome heat flashed through his system. One of want and need—and intrigue. The woman was magnificent, even while muddy and still wet. "Sheriff?" He turned to the man glaring at him. "Kiss my ass." With less class than his woman had shown, he shoved the deputies out of his way and strode after her.

Now all he had to do was convince her that he had to protect her.

Yeah. What could go wrong with that conversation? He sighed and followed her into the early morning outside the station. "Mariana? Wait up."

"No," she snapped, jumping into the one taxi in town. A second later, it sped off.

He watched it go. Fine. There was something she didn't know about him, and he'd easily beat her home. Let's see how she liked that since there was definitely something about him she could never know.

Who, or rather what, he truly was.

Vampire.

Chapter 4

Mariana dressed in yoga pants and an over-large sweatshirt before tugging thick comfy socks over her chilled feet. She'd remained in the shower until the water had turned lukewarm, and now she was clean of mud. Her hair was drying around her face, and she needed breakfast. Did she have eggs? Humming, she strode from her bedroom into the living room and stopped cold.

Raine Maxwell sat on her floor, legs extended, head back on the wall and his eyes closed. A duffel bag sat next to him. Mud covered his motorcycle boots and the bottom of his jeans, which had dried nicely to show the muscles in his thighs.

She caught her breath. "What are you doing here?"

He slowly opened his eyes but didn't move otherwise. "I figured we should talk."

Seriously? She looked at her locked front door. "How did you get inside?" Her gun was still in the kitchen. Why hadn't she taken it into the bathroom with her?

"It's a talent." He watched her like she was something curious and slightly yummy. As if he wanted to play and then eat.

Her shiver wasn't all about fear. Maybe not much about fear. "Tell me once and for all," she murmured.

"I'm not your damn stalker." He rolled his eyes. "Give me a break, Doc. You know I'm not."

Every instinct in her body told her he wasn't the stalker from Dallas. "You might not be the main stalker, but here you are, breaking and entering." Thank goodness she'd gotten dressed after her shower. She'd lived alone for so long that walking around in a towel wasn't a big deal.

"I didn't break, but I did enter." He rolled his neck, finally moving. "The window lock is flimsy in your guest room, and it didn't take much to jimmy it open. I'll fix that for you later today."

She put her hands on her hips. "That lock was fine, and I had a wedge in the sill."

His eyebrows rose. "No wedge. Interesting. I thought you said the guy came in from the garage."

"He did." The memory of the kidnapping would haunt her until they caught this guy or his team. "The wedge is really gone?"

"Yeah," Raine said softly. "Somebody removed that wedge from the sill—and the only reason would be so they could return and get inside easily. Look around the house and make sure nothing else is missing."

This wasn't making any sense. The kidnapper had thrown her in a trunk and driven away. Had his partner gone through her house? Bile spiraled through her stomach. "The stalker went through my home," she whispered. After his buddy had taken her, he'd spent time in her house? She rubbed her arms, suddenly chilled. Definitely violated.

"It's okay." Raine stretched to his feet, looking formidable and dangerous. "I meant what I said. We're going to figure out who this guy is, I'm going to take care of him, and you're going to be fine."

Her mouth went dry. Bone dry. "Take care of him? You mean you're going to turn him in to the police, right?" Hopefully Evan O'Connell would be sheriff by then.

"Right," Raine said, a veil over his eyes again. "Here's the plan. I'm going to take a quick shower and change clothes. While I'm doing that, you search your house and see if he took anything. If you need me, yell and I'll be right by your side. Then we'll make breakfast and come up with a plan."

A naked Raine Maxwell in her shower? Yeah, those chills dissipated quickly. "Why don't you go home to shower?"

"I don't have a place in Indiana," he admitted. "I gave up my lease on the condo when I left town."

Her chin lifted. This was all too much—and so was he. He was sexy and dangerous and unfathomable. She didn't know him, and she shouldn't trust him. Not yet, anyway. "Then go to a hotel."

"No." He turned and prowled into her guest room, walking right to the small adjoining bathroom, where he shut the door.

She gaped at the empty doorway. No? He couldn't just say 'no.' Oh, she should call the sheriff and have him arrested for trespassing, but the sheriff was a dolt. Kind of. He'd impressed her with some of his questions and reasoning, but right now, she was on her own.

Well, on her own with Raine Maxwell. She'd never admit it to him, but she felt much safer with him around. Of course, right now he was naked in her guest bathroom.

Her body did a whole tremble top to bottom at the thought.

Oh, this was a disaster.

* * * *

After a long shower where he figured Mariana could come to the conclusion that she wanted him around for now, Raine pulled on a fresh pair of faded jeans and a black sweater he'd stolen from his brother a year ago. It fit him better, anyway. Finger combing his hair, he padded barefoot out of the room and into the living room, where he caught sight of a small gathering in the kitchen. "What the heck?"

Evan McConnell looked up from the table, his cop eyes appraising. "Heard you got darted."

His mate and fiancée, Tabi Rusko, snorted in delicate laughter. "That's hilarious." Tabi was a full demoness who'd mated Evan just a couple of months before, and so far, Evan seemed to be doing okay with going from human to immortal. The situation was incredibly rare when the human was male, and often they were too volatile or dangerous.

Raine didn't want him around Mariana at the moment, just in case. "How are you feeling, Evan?" he drawled.

"Stronger than ever." The cop's brown eyes sparkled. "If you know what I mean."

Yeah. He certainly did. Raine rocked back on his heels and noticed a place set for him next to Mariana. She dished him a plate of scrambled eggs and bacon.

"I couldn't wait," she murmured. "After calling in these two, I made breakfast."

Tabi tipped back her mimosa. "I vouched for you, so stop looking so grumpy. There's no way you're a stalker or that you kidnapped anybody." Her white-blond hair was in a ponytail, and her black eyes danced with amusement. The few pure-bred demonesses alive had similar coloring and were notoriously petite...and slightly nuts.

Even so, Raine's spirits lifted. "Thank you." He should've thought of calling in Tabi for a character reference. While they hadn't known each other long, she was a sweetheart and from his world—and Mariana seemed to like and trust her.

"Sure." Tabi snagged a piece of bacon from her mate's plate. "I'm sure Abby and Noah would vouch for you, but they're still in the Caribbean."

Evan munched happily on a bagel. "They needed the vacation but will return to help with the final week of the campaign in a few days."

Oh, they'd definitely needed a vacation. Noah was a hybrid who'd mated Abby and defended her from a psycho ex by killing him. "Has the sheriff still been harassing them about her ex's death?" The sheriff had tried to pin the death on Abby, considering her scumbag ex had been a friend.

Evan's mouth flattened out. "Yeah. We have to get him out of office."

It was difficult not talking about real life, but Mariana couldn't know about immortals. So Raine took his seat and dug into the eggs. They were delicious.

Evan leaned back. "Mariana told us about the kidnapping, and I'm so sorry I missed her call about the roses being left on her porch. What's your take on it, Raine?"

Raine chewed thoughtfully. "I don't know. The sedative was a strong one." In other words, it had taken down a four-hundred-year-old hybrid, so it was possible the enemy was immortal and knew exactly who he was.

Tabi reached for the champagne bottle to refill her glass. "There are several horse tranquilizers that could've been used. Strong ones."

If that was the situation, then maybe the jerk was human and had just gotten lucky with the drug. "If that's the case, they didn't care if they killed me," Raine mused. The quantity probably would've killed a human.

Mariana jolted. "How can you sound so casual about that? You could've *died*." She reached out and planted her small hand on his.

The soft touch wound right through his body to the beast at his core, and the damn creature roared. Raine forced a smile. "I didn't die, so let's not worry about that." It took every ounce of his control not to flip his hand over and capture hers.

Evan watched him. "Do you have any enemies we need to know about?"

Mariana jumped. "Don't be silly. This was about me and that stupid stalker I can't get rid of. He took the safety wedge out of my guest window so he can come back. Nothing else is missing, though." She looked down at her still full champagne glass and removed her hand.

"We'll get a new lock and wedge for the window." Raine said, the hair rising on the back of his neck.

She paled. "I know, but it's driving me crazy that I can't figure out who this guy is."

Raine caught an expletive before it emerged. Anger tornadoed through him, and he took another bite of eggs, but now they tasted like dust. He hid his expression until he could clear it. "We will find him."

Evan drank some water. "Raine, I agree, but is there anybody in your life who might think you're destined and have gone after her?"

Mariana choked and reached for water to drink. She set the glass back down. "Destined? Evan, that's crazy."

Except it wasn't. Not at all. Raine sighed and reached for the champagne. Why not? "No. None of my enemies would think I have a destiny or would seek out Mariana."

She looked at him like he was nuts. "You guys are missing the boat here about the stalker. He would think that he's *my* destiny."

Tabi chuckled and drank more champagne. Oh, the demoness loved seeing other people in difficult situations. There was no doubt if they all voted, she'd choose to just tell Mariana everything, which would break the most important law of every species and coalition. "That's such a good point, Mariana," she drawled in her husky voice. "But some of us do believe in fate. What about you, Raine?"

Oh, he was going to smack the demoness. Except that he kind of liked her, even though she was a pain. "No, but I do believe in action." He finished his drink. "Mariana? Do you have copies of the case files from Dallas? We need to find this guy before he goes for you again."

She nodded. "I have everything in the desk in the guest room. The Dallas police did everything they could to find him, but he stayed under the radar."

Raine sat back. "Good. I have a brother who's an expert technical analyst. We'll have him take a look." Cade could find anybody.

Tabi sat up. "Ohhh. The mysterious Maxwell clan starts to take shape."

Mariana looked at her. "Huh?"

Raine placed his hand over hers this time, partially to distract her and mostly to appease his own need. "Also, I need to bring the rest of my stuff in from the truck."

She blinked. "Why?"

"Because I'm moving in until this guy is caught." Raine pointedly ignored Evan's narrowing of eyes, Tabi's smile of delight, and Mariana's look of pure argument.

Why hadn't he just stayed in Montana? Oh yeah. He was dying. Until now that he was next to Mariana. He sighed.

Tabi laughed.

Chapter 5

Mariana stared at the murder board Raine had created across the wall of the guest room. Dates, times, theories—all of them from the Dallas Police Department.

"We really don't have much," Raine said, leaning back against the wall. "I've sent everything to my brother, and maybe he'll be able to come up with something the cops couldn't. If anybody can retrieve the video from your cameras, it'd be Cade." He rolled his neck, and the muscles bunched in his upper arms.

Mariana tried to swallow and wet her suddenly dry throat. Having him near was too much for her libido, and if the guy had any idea of the dreams he'd starred in lately, he'd probably blush. Well, maybe. Something told her that Raine didn't blush. "Why did you leave town?" she asked.

One of his brows arched. How could a freakin' eyebrow look sexy? "The job was done."

Ouch. Okay. Well, then. He'd only been there for the job of watching Ivar and Noah. "Then why did you come back?" She looked away from him.

His sigh was long-suffering and didn't tell her a thing. "That's a long story, and I can't go into it."

"Seriously?" She whipped around to face him. "Are you kidding me? You show up on my porch, get kidnapped, admit you were in my group under false pretenses, take off for Montana, and then return without being able to explain why? Oh, I don't think so. Either you start talking right now or you get the heck out of my house." The place already seemed smaller and somehow safer with him in it, but she knew better than to start depending on him. He'd be gone again soon.

His eyes flared in a way that didn't even look human. "I'm out of here the second we find this guy."

Yikes. Okay. That hurt a little bit. She'd thought she'd gotten an interested vibe from him a couple of times, but maybe she'd misread him? He was the sexiest man she'd ever been this close to in real life, so maybe he went for perfection like Tabi Rusko? Mariana was fine with her curves and looks, but maybe she'd overestimated Raine's interest when he'd thrown Johnny Baker up against the wall after the kid had insulted her. "I think you should leave."

"No."

Heat flashed up her spine to tingle at her nape. "No? Are you joking?"

"No." He cocked his head, watching her.

She had the strongest urge to punch him again, but her wrist still ached from last time. The guy had abs of solid rock. "I don't think you're understanding me," she gritted out.

He moved toward her without warning, pivoting and putting her back against the wall. "You're not understanding me." His big body loomed over her, and an unexpected heat rolled off him.

She cleared her throat, forcing herself to stare him right in the eyes. "I don't go for the alpha-male act, dickhead."

His smile was slow and held enough warning that she stopped breathing. "Oh, sweetheart. Don't play games with me, and don't lie to either one of us. You're as aroused right now as I am, and you should definitely understand that this isn't an act."

What was happening? He'd gone from distant to right in her space without a hint. Confusion and desire clouded through her, mixing into a potent blend that sprang her nerves wide awake and alive. "Back up."

"No," he said, even softer this time.

Her head jerked. "You can't say 'no.'"

"I just did." He waited patiently, danger stamped hard on his face. "Are you done with the nonsense?"

Who the hell did this jackass think he was? Yeah, he was sexy and somehow turning her on, but enough was enough. "I think you're stuck in the dark ages, buddy," she gritted out, acutely aware that tingles were still spreading throughout her body.

"You have no idea," he agreed, humor lighting his eyes to a seafoam green to mix with the desire glittering there. "Whoever kidnapped us is now my enemy, and your safety is my utmost concern anyway. So I stay here until you're safe. Period."

She wanted to be safe. She also wanted to be in control of this situation, and he'd grabbed it with both hands. "I don't like being bossed around."

"I'll keep that in mind," he said quietly. "Are we good now?"

"No." She crossed her arms, so warm from his near body that she wanted to slide right against him. "Why am I your utmost concern?"

He stepped back, taking his warmth with him. "That's a good question and a fair one."

She rubbed her now chilling arms. "Then answer it."

For a moment, he looked like he really wanted to tell her something. Then that darn veil dropped over his eyes. "It's better if you don't know."

"That's stupid," she exploded. "And confusing and it doesn't make sense."

"I know," he said, crossing his arms. His very cut, ripped, and muscled arms.

She couldn't stop looking at those muscles. "Right when you got back, you seemed pale and, well, smaller." His two weeks away had somehow seemed to make him ill. How had that happened? "But you look fine now and right back to full strength. Are you on medication that you stopped taking when you went to Montana?" It was the only thing that made an iota of sense.

"Kind of," he allowed.

"Why would you stop taking your meds?" What was wrong with him? She hated secrets.

He sighed. "Because taking my meds leads to danger and complications."

Oh. She took a deep breath. The changes in him had been physical, so what could that be? "I'm not saying you can stay here, because I haven't decided. But if you do, you have to level with me about your condition. I need to know what it is, what I can do, and what the side effects are for the medication you seem to be taking again. Start talking, please."

He sighed. "No."

* * * *

The woman socked him right in the abs again and then looked stricken. "Oh, God. I'm sorry. Are you okay?" she whispered. "I forgot you have an illness."

"I do not have an illness." He frowned. "I didn't even feel your punch. Is your hand injured?"

She shook it out. "You're driving me crazy."

"Now you know how I feel," he returned, grasping her hand and turning it over to see her knuckles already bruising. "You are a delicate one, now aren't you?"

She pulled away. "No. Tell me what's wrong with you, or I'm going to take my chances with the sheriff. I don't want to go that route, and I'm sure you agree, so start talking."

Right. If he told her he was an immortal vampire with a hint of demon in his lineage, she'd call the sheriff in two hot seconds to have him committed. Oh, he could prove it to her, but what then? He sighed and ran a rough hand through his thick hair. "Can't you just trust me?"

She frowned and reached for his hand. "When did you get a tattoo?"

The second he'd met her, actually. He looked down at the M marking on his right palm—M for his last name, Maxwell. The Maxwell crest was jagged and rough—showing both Celtic and Nordic ancestry and the dangers of having both. The barbs extending from the brutal 'M' showed his strength…and his curse. After finding out about her, he'd instantly headed to Dallas for just one look. Then he'd stood close to her in a silly coffee shop, and the branding mark had instantly appeared. "It's a long story," he murmured.

"Isn't everything with you?" She leaned over for a better look at his brand, and the damn thing started to heat to a temperature that drummed energy through his veins.

Oh, he'd watched her and fallen hard. She had a sharp wit and a kind heart to go with an obvious beauty that hit him square center. The muscles bunched down his back with the hunger to take her to the floor. The female had no idea what she was unleashing by just touching him. "Mariana? That's just a family crest and nothing else." He nearly choked on the lie. The brand darkened before his eyes, so near to her flesh. To her soft, silky skin that he could possess with the rest of her. The vampire, or maybe demon, strength in his body soared to the surface, let free once again. For now.

She pressed her thumb to the brand and nearly dropped him to his knees.

Fire, hunger, lust all rushed through him so quickly he didn't have time to grab control. Instead, he grabbed her. Fast and rough, he lifted her against the wall and moved in, taking her mouth in a way he'd dreamed about since the first day they'd met.

She did taste like peaches.

He dove deep, pressing her to the wall and plastering his hard body against her soft one. So much softness combined with sweetness.

She moaned, and her hands dug into his hair as she returned the kiss.

He wrapped an arm around her waist, dragging her harder against him while the other hand went through her silky hair to cup her head and hold her where he needed her. He kissed her, taking her taste and sweetness into him, letting her soft moans drown out the roaring in his head.

In his body.

The kiss consumed him in this small space where only they existed, but every predatory instinct he had spiraled out from the two of them, seeking for threats in a natural way most people used to breathe. The primal being at his core held her close, tasting her, finally appeased that she was right where she should be.

Where they both should be.

The marking on his palm cut deep with an insistent drum that he mark her—that he mate her. Only Mariana, no matter the cost.

At the thought—the only thought that would bring him back to reality—he lifted his head. Her eyes had darkened while a lovely peach flush covered her high cheekbones and matched her now slightly bruised mouth. A mouth he wanted to take again. Right now. "I want you," he said.

Humor melded with the need in her eyes. "Yeah. I got that." She didn't attempt to draw away.

How could she make him want to smile and tear off her clothing at the same time? "I'm dying." Shit. He hadn't meant to blurt it out like that.

She blinked and then stiffened. "You're what?"

He tried to release her head, but her hair had tangled around his fingers. "Hold on." He gently wound the stands free and was careful to keep from hurting her. Then he stepped back, releasing her completely. She'd gone pale. "It's not contagious," he hastened to explain.

She barely shook her head. "Wait a minute. How are you dying?"

"Huh." He shouldn't blurt things out. "It's a genetic disease with no cure." That was partly true. It was definitely genetic, and the cure wasn't one he'd pursue.

"What kind of genetic disease?" She was all business now.

He lifted one shoulder. "We call it the Maxwell Curse." At least that was the truth. "It affects every Maxwell male." Considering he had vampire blood in his veins, he could only have boys.

"It's a family disease?" She tapped a finger on her bottom lip. "I have a friend from my golf league who's a geneticist in Dallas. Have you gotten second opinions on this? There's so much we can do with genetics these days."

"You golf?"

"Yes. Well, I did in Dallas. I'll probably join a league here when I finish getting settled." She frowned. "You didn't distract me from my question, by the way. Have you gotten a second opinion on your genetic disease?"

"Yeah. There's nothing that can be done." The last thing he could do was have his genes sampled and studied by a human. He and whatever scientist he hired would be dead before the needle was even drawn out of his arm and probably with a good deal of pain first. That much he knew for sure. "We have met with a doctor during the last couple of years, and she's working on it, but we have no answers." Dr. Faith Cooper was mated to an immortal while not being part of the Realm, which was a coalition of species. His family couldn't go to the Realm with this information, but he trusted Faith Cooper—because Benny trusted her.

Mariana looked him up and down. "You seem strong with good color, and your eyes are clear. What exactly happens with this genetic mutation?"

"I die," he said simply. "We live to a certain age and then our bodies break down. I haven't studied it and just worked on living a full life to this point."

She grabbed his harm and dug her nails in. "You haven't studied it? Come on. That's crazy. You're what? I'd say you're around thirty, but your eyes look older. Maybe thirty-five? How can you just start tearing down at this age? I've never heard of a disease or mutation like that."

He liked her hand on him. A lot. "We don't really go around advertising it. I just wanted you to know."

She looked up at him, confusion and suspicion now replacing the need in her pretty eyes. "Why?"

"So when I asked if you wanted to have a brief affair, you'd know that I meant it."

Chapter 6

Mariana would've stepped back, but her rear was already flush to the wall. "Get the hell out of my house."

Raine didn't so much as twitch. "What?"

She sidled by him and exited the room, heading straight for her kitchen and a glass of wine. "You're dying? Seriously?" Anger flicked down her back and heated her skin on the way. Just how stupid did he think she was? Yeah, she'd pegged him for a player from day one, and she'd been right. "Get out of my house. Now."

He followed her in that sexy lope he had. "I don't understand."

She flipped around to face him, and her body was still on fire, damn it. "You're dying so we need to fuck a few nights and then you're gone? You just wanted me to know all the details?" The sarcasm on her tongue almost burned. "That has got to be the worst line I've heard in my entire life, and I've heard a couple of doozies before."

He scratched his whiskered chin and eyed her like she was unstable. "It's the truth."

"Right," she drawled, turning back for the already open bottle of 2017 La Carrodilla Syrah on the counter. "If you don't leave now, I'm calling the moron sheriff. At least he doesn't act like I'm stupid." The worst part was that they'd been headed to the bed if Raine hadn't pulled this jackass move. She'd wanted him, and she probably would've said yes.

Raine's phone rang in his back pocket, and he pulled it out to press to his ear. "Raine here." He paused and listened. "Hi, Grams. Yes, I know." Then he quieted as he listened for almost a minute. "Yes. I understand." He sounded patient and stubborn at the same time. "But I—" He became quiet again and then pinched the bridge of his nose. "Yes. Okay. Love you, too. Bye." He put the phone back into place.

Mariana crossed her arms. "You're telling me that was actually your grandmother."

"Yes." He rubbed his forehead as if a headache loomed. "She was just checking in."

The guy made no sense. He propositioned her after giving the worst line ever, and then he talked to his grandmother like a nice person? "It sounded like she was giving you the business," Mariana observed, pouring herself a glass of wine.

"You could say that." Raine tucked his thumbs in his pockets.

"About what?" Mariana inhaled the fragrant wine and then took a testing sip.

He shook his head.

"Is she concerned about your impending death?" Mariana drawled, her lips still tingling from his kiss.

His gaze sharpened to emerald blades. "Yes."

Right. Maybe he was crazy. It was sad, but she'd rather he was nuts than purposefully trying to manipulate her. She could deal with nuts. Assholish was beyond her level of expertise. "Then you should probably go back to Montana or wherever your family is and spend your last days with them."

"I don't much care for your sarcasm," he said, sounding more thoughtful than irritated.

"That's easy to remedy." She took another drink of the wine. "Get out of my house."

His stance remained relaxed. "I thought I'd take care of your stalker before leaving."

Oh yeah. "You're my great protector, now aren't you?" She studied him and tried to see beneath the too handsome exterior. What if he had engineered her kidnapping? She had trusted him until he came up with the dying ruse. How could he be dying? He looked perfectly healthy, and if a genetic mutation was so prevalent it killed all males in his family, there would've been some research conducted. "How exactly are you going to die?" She sipped more.

He blinked. "I slowly get weaker and then my brain stops functioning."

Yeah, he was full of crap. "So somebody has to pull the plug, huh?" The wine was good. She should stock up on more.

"In a manner of speaking." He cocked his head. "You don't believe me, and I guess I don't blame you for that. How about we forget the last hour and go back to trying to find this stalker before I leave town?"

"That plan no longer works for me." She swirled the liquid in the glass. "Either you're deranged or you're a moron, so I don't want your help. I do, however, want you to leave." It was too bad he was the sexiest man she'd ever met.

"Deranged or a moron? How do you figure?" His drawl held the slightest bit of warning.

She sighed. "You're deranged if you believe your story, and you're a moron if you think I'll fall for it. Either way, I'll handle the stalker without you." Why hadn't he pulled this crap after they'd had a night together? Based on that one kiss, it would've been a night to remember. "There are several good shrinks I can refer you to."

"You're the only shrink I want," he drawled.

Her lungs compressed, and her nipples sharpened. Just from one sexy statement from him. Maybe *she* needed the shrink. Enough of this. She drew her phone from the counter. "Leave or I call the police. It's up to you."

"Fine." He whipped his phone out and dialed a number, waiting until somebody answered. "Hi. I'm calling in my favor." His tone lowered to gritty. "Yeah. Now. I need Faith to talk to Mariana and tell her I'm not full of shit. Yes—within those perimeters. Of course. Thank you." He handed the phone over.

Mariana gingerly accepted it. "Hello?"

"Just a sec," a familiar voice boomed. "Hey, Doc Lopez. How are things? This is Benny."

Benny? Mariana set her glass down. "How are you?" He'd only shown up at the group meeting to pick up Ivar, but the mammoth man made an impression. "And why are you involved in this?"

"Oh, I owe Maxwell a favor, and if all I have to do is hand the phone to Faith, then hey. Why not?" He sounded like he was walking outside in the rain.

"Who's Faith?" Mariana asked, her head reeling. This was all too weird. Way odd.

Benny chuckled. "That's a good question. Faith is a pretty famous neurosurgeon or something like that. She's the only doctor Raine and his family trust enough to consult with. You could look her up if you want. Dr. Faith Cooper."

Mariana moved for the laptop on her kitchen table and flipped it open to research the doctor. The woman was impressive and had published several papers as well as worked at several different hospitals, most recently in Denver. She was now working in the private sector but didn't have any forwarding information.

Muffled voices came over the line before a women's voice cleared. "Hello? This is Dr. Cooper." She sounded curious.

"Um, hi. This is Dr. Lopez, and I'm wondering how I'm supposed to believe that you're Dr. Cooper." Mariana tilted her head to the side to watch Raine. This whole afternoon was spiraling out of control.

The woman laughed. "Well, that's easy. Flip on the video conference."

Mariana paused. She should've thought of that. "Okay." She started the camera, and a beautiful woman with soft brown eyes and long brown hair came into view. Mariana compared the woman in the phone to a picture of Dr. Cooper online, and then spent about thirty minutes questioning the woman about neurology, some of the papers she'd written, and other tidbits. By the end of the time, Mariana was convinced the woman on the phone was Dr. Cooper. "Sorry about the inquisition," she murmured.

Faith laughed. "No problem. Hearing that there's yet another unknown genetic mutation that causes death is common, but hearing there's one that causes a male like Raine to die quickly has to make you suspicious. I don't blame you."

Mariana sat back at her table. "So it's true? I don't see how."

Faith was dressed in a pretty yellow sweater that contrasted with the rain falling outside the window behind her. "The Maxwell Curse is a little like Huntington's disease, where a person is healthy until the disease takes effect—usually in the thirties or forties. Or Alzheimer's, which doesn't attack until later in life. But for those inflicted with Maxwell's, the decline is rapid once symptoms appear."

Holy crap. Nausea rolled through Mariana's stomach. She was such an asshole. "I thought he was making it up as a come-on," she whispered.

Faith winced. "Yeah, it does sound crazy if you were looking at him, because he looks so healthy. But the decline will be rapid unless he gets the cure."

Mariana stiffened. "There's a cure?"

Faith blanched. "There's a treatment, I guess. Not really a cure. But sometimes the treatment causes more complications than the disease, and I'm sure Raine is concerned about that."

"What's the treatment?" Mariana asked, ignoring the man now lounging on her sofa and flipping through channels to a soccer game.

Faith grimaced. "That's all I've been cleared to tell you. HIPAA laws and all of that. You'll have to get more information from Raine, and I think you should. You really should."

"Hey. Enough with my phone." Benny came into focus. "I have a mission to do, and I'm going now. I hope you found your answers, Lopez. If not, punch Raine a few times and make him tell you everything. I swear. Why does everyone have to make every damn situation so difficult these days? Fate matters. When you find the one, you—" The phone went dead.

Mariana stared at the blank screen. "I think somebody disengaged the call. What was Benny talking about?"

Raine didn't look away from the soccer match. "Benjamin Reese is a quart low of a full tank, if you know what I mean. He's slightly nutty but a great guy in a fight—so long as he remembers who's on his side."

Mariana left her phone in place and poured two glasses of wine this time, taking one over to Raine on the sofa. "I owe you an apology."

He took the glass. "Don't worry about it."

She gingerly touched his arm and waited until he turned to face her. "I'm very sorry I made light of your illness. Honestly, I thought you were lying. It all seems so bizarre." But comparing the genetic illness to Huntington's or Alzheimer's did bring the reality home. "I don't want you to die."

His lip quirked. "Sorry. Now you have to be the one to pull the plug."

She dropped her head. "I'm sorry."

"I was just kidding. Don't worry about it. I understand that it's all crazy, and since I'm not telling you some details, I'm sure this doesn't make sense. I don't want to die, believe me. But I think I made the most of what time I was given."

She set down her full wineglass. "What's the treatment you don't want to try?" If she was in the same boat, she'd probably try any treatment to stay alive, unless it was so horrible it wasn't worth it.

He shook his head. "Doesn't matter. I'm not going to use the treatment, so there's no reason to discuss it."

She leaned into him as one of the teams scored a goal and the crowd went nuts on the television. "Is the treatment painful? Experimental?"

He rubbed his knuckle along her jawline, sending nice tingles through her face. "Can we not discuss this any longer? I don't like talking about any of this, and honestly, this is as open as I've been in a long while. Let's just enjoy a few moments of wine and a game, and then we can get back to your case. I really do want to take this stalker out before I have to head home." He turned to her, set an arm over her shoulders, and tugged her against him.

She stiffened for the briefest of seconds and then snuggled into his side. It felt right. *They* felt right. Why couldn't she take time to explore this? "Please tell me about the treatments. Maybe there's something I could do."

His chest moved as he chuckled. "How about you just relax and enjoy the moment with me?" Then he leaned them both over and reclaimed her wine glass to set in her hand before settling back.

It wasn't too much for him to ask. "Okay. One more question. You said the disease only affects male members of your family. Do you have any brothers and have they already gone through this?" She took a sip of the drink, her mind still reeling.

"Yeah. I have six brothers, and I'm the oldest. The disease has hit me first in this generation." He kissed the top of her head and then kicked his legs out to relax. "My offer of sex as we work this case is still on the table."

She choked on her wine even as her body perked right up.

The doorbell rang, and she jumped. "I'll get it."

"No." He released her and set his wine down. "I've got it." He stretched to his feet, appearing so healthy and virile that it hurt to look at him.

She peered over her shoulder at the door when he opened it and paused.

"Who are these from?" he asked.

Her stomach dropped, and she craned her neck to see better. A teenager handed Raine a bouquet of at least three dozen white roses.

The kid shrugged. "I'm just the delivery guy, but there is a card."

Raine tipped him and then shut the door, looking at the roses. He tugged out a card and flipped it open. His jaw clenched.

"What does it say?" Mariana whispered.

He looked up, and his eyes burned a bright green. "It says: *Mariana, I'm sorry our date was interrupted. I'll see you soon.*"

Chapter 7

Raine sensed the demoness before he saw her. After pacing the kitchen for about an hour, the hair on the back of his neck stood up. He paused and looked toward his bedroom. Sighing, he turned and walked inside the room, shutting the door. "What the hell are you doing here?"

Tabi sat on his bed, her legs crossed at the ankles of shiny boots. Her white-blond hair was wet from the rain, but a raincoat had been placed over the deckchair, so at least she wasn't getting the bed wet. The window remained open to show the darkened night. "You smelled off earlier today, and I couldn't stop thinking about it." Her black eyes appraised him. "You're still off. Like an ill human. I'm confused."

Well. All he needed was to deal with a confused and slightly crazy demoness. "Where's your mate?" he asked, looking toward the darkened night.

"Right here." Evan came into view through the window, standing right outside. "I was scouting the area and didn't feel comfortable infiltrating your bedroom." He gave his mate a look.

Raine couldn't help the grin. "I appreciate the kindness, Evan. Want to tell me what your mate is doing on my bed?"

Tabi sighed. "What's wrong with you? Vampires don't get sick, and neither do demons, and yet..." She delicately sniffed the air and then her gaze pinpointed on his neck. "I'll read your mind if I have to, but I'll need to attack it to get in. Sure you want me to do that?"

Evan put his hand on the sill as rain dropped onto his hair. "There will be no demon mind attacks, Tabitha."

The demoness pouted.

Raine smiled his thanks at his friend. Oh, it wasn't as if Tabi had an obedient bone in her body. Rather, Evan had the ability to shield his mind and others from a mind attack, and apparently he was willing to do so for Raine. "I appreciate it. Sure am glad you mated the demoness here. How's immortality going for you, E?" When an enhanced human mated an immortal, their chromosomal pairs increased to immortality. An enhanced human male was a feared anomaly because of the sudden strength and power.

Evan shrugged. "I feel better than I did as human, but I did accidentally break a window by sneezing the other day."

Tabi sighed. "We're keeping him under wraps to avoid the multitude of assassins that would come out of the woodwork. I swear, I had no idea it was so rare to find somebody like Evan. But we're handling it, just like we'll handle whatever is going on with you. Start talking, Raine."

"Can't. Blood oath," he said quietly, knowing a demon would back off.

"Too bad. I can smell illness, and that makes zero sense," she returned, power all but cascading from her. "I will fry your mind."

Evan sighed. "No, you won't. I already have him shielded, so stop pushing against my mind. It isn't nice, Tab. If Raine wants privacy, we're going to give it to him."

Yep. Even as a deadly emerging immortal, the ex-cop was a good guy. Raine forced a smile. "I'm fine, Tabi. If and when I need help, I will call you immediately. Right now, I have to keep my vow of silence. Besides, there isn't anything else you can do." He glanced pointedly at his watch. "It's after midnight, and I need sleep." Mariana had gone to bed at least an hour or so before. "Thanks for visiting."

Tabi crossed her arms over her chest. "I am not leaving until you tell us what's going on."

Raine didn't want to fight with her, and he really didn't want to take on Evan right now. "Later, Tabs. Give me some time."

Evan motioned her toward the window. "All right, sweetheart. Give the guy a break." He looked at the wall behind Raine. "Any luck with the stalker?"

"No. He sent more roses today but used an online form. The IP address traced back to the local library." Raine was going to owe more favors after the ones he'd called in today, but he was fine with that. "I had a friend hack into the surveillance system at the library, and turns out there isn't one."

Evan's eyebrows lifted. "When I become sheriff, I'll start taking a look at surveillance in town. We need some CCTV in areas like that, just to keep people safe."

Tabi sat up. "So the stalker guy is here. Good. Let's find him and rip off his head."

"That's my plan," Raine agreed. Mariana had turned an alarming pale shade when the roses had arrived. "She's scared, and I don't know how to reassure her that she'll be okay." Especially since now she knew that his time was limited. "I want to tell her about me, about us, but…"

Tabi bit her lip. "You can't unless you mate her. I've seen the mating mark on your hand. What's the problem?" When a demon met his or her mate, their marking appeared so it could transfer during the mating.

The problem was that he was dying and he couldn't ask her to give up her life so he could live.

"Tabi—enough," Evan said. "Let's go. It's starting to rain harder."

Tabi turned her gaze on her mate through the open window. "You're immortal now. Rain won't hurt you."

"Tabs." Evan's gaze darkened. "Let's. Go."

Interesting. While Tabi had the strength of her species, Evan was unreal. It'd be interesting to see them wrestle a bit, because Evan would probably win. However, he was still concerned and careful with his newfound strength, and Tabi would definitely take advantage of that. Raine changed his mind. He didn't want to see them destroy Mariana's house. "Thank you for your concern, and I will definitely be in touch."

Tabi rolled her eyes but at least got off his bed and headed for the window. "I'm not done with this."

Evan lifted her out. "I didn't think you were." He looked back at Raine. "I've gotten you a brief reprieve. Good luck." He shut the window and they disappeared.

Luck? There was no such thing.

* * * *

A loud bang jerked Mariana from a nightmare where white roses drowned her. She sat up, gasping. Another bang, this one an explosion, ripped through the night.

Her door flew open. "Mariana?" Raine stood there, outlined by the faint light from the kitchen.

Another explosion boomed, and something hit the side of the house.

She jumped out of bed and ran toward him. "What is going on?"

He slipped a gun into her hand and drew her into the living room, pulling them toward the front door. Keeping her behind him, he opened it.

Heat and the sound of crackling fire hit her first. "Raine?" She held the gun in her right hand and placed her left against his warm and bare back.

"It's my truck." He stepped out onto the porch and looked around before lifting his head and sniffing. "I don't see or sense anybody near." He paused and didn't move for several seconds, watching whatever was right in front of him. Sirens sounded in the distance.

She slipped to his side to see spirals of fire and smoke coming from inside his silver truck, which was parked at the curb. Silver paint bubbled on the outside door, and the hood crashed open with another explosion.

Raine turned and covered her as heat washed over them.

Tires skidded to a stop outside. Mariana peered around him to see two firetrucks followed by several other emergency vehicles.

"Go get dressed," Raine said, prodding her toward her bedroom. "Whoever did this is gone. Just hurry."

She turned and ran into her bedroom, yanking on jeans and a sweater before securing her hair into a ponytail. Male voices were already mingling when she made her way back to the living room, where Raine sat on her sofa with Sheriff Baker and his son in the chairs across the coffee table.

The sheriff looked up when she entered. "Are you okay?"

She nodded and took the vacant seat by Raine. "Yes." Then she angled her neck to see out the window where the firefighters were just rolling up the hoses. Smoke still poured from the demolished truck. "Is the fire out?"

"Yes," Raine said, feeling solid and strong next to her. He'd pulled on jeans earlier but was still bare chested without socks.

The door opened and the fire marshal poked his head in. "Looks like a couple of Molotov cocktails though the driver's side window. Saw remains of burned glass on the floor, and we'll have our expert out here to take a look soon."

"Thanks," the sheriff said, his gaze remaining on her. "Mr. Maxwell? Is there anything you'd like to tell us?"

Raine arched one eyebrow. "Considering somebody just bombed my truck, I was hoping you'd have some insight. *Sheriff.*"

"Who are your enemies?" the sheriff barked.

"Don't have any," Raine barked right back.

Johnny kept staring at Mariana, and his beady eyes had narrowed more than usual. "Isn't it a crime to sleep with one of your patients, Dr. Lopez?" He emphasized the title with just enough derision that Mariana's temper slid into the fear and confusion.

"Watch it, junior," Raine said, the implicit warning all the more frightening for how quiet his voice remained. "I threw you against a wall once, and I'm more than happy to do it again."

Johnny didn't look away from Mariana. Apparently the guy wasn't smart enough to keep his focus on the biggest threat.

The sheriff hitched himself up. "Was that a threat against a law enforcement officer?"

Mariana hastened to stop the oncoming disaster. "Sheriff, I have a stalker, as you know. I'm sure this bombing was an attack by him. Have you contacted the Dallas police force?"

"I have, and they're sending copies of the casefile tomorrow," the sheriff said. "However, since this bombing was against Mr. Maxwell, we really need to look at any enemies he no doubt has."

"Nope. Everyone loves me," Raine said, extending his arm along the back of the sofa and resting his hand on Mariana's shoulder in a move that spoke volumes. His fingers tapped against her neck as if he had every right to do so while his expression remained casual and rather amused.

Both the sheriff and his son looked pointedly at the hand on her shoulder.

She wanted to tell them all to get lost, but at the moment, she'd take Raine's support over either of theirs. Especially since she didn't understand this illness of his. Would it attack suddenly? Were there actual attacks? She should've asked more questions the night before, but he was so good at deflecting. Was he embarrassed to be ill? He sure didn't look embarrassed.

"Well?" Johnny asked.

Crap. She hadn't been listening. "Well what?" she asked.

The sheriff frowned. "I offered to take you into protective custody. Just you and right now."

"She's staying here," Raine said quietly. "I can protect her."

"Obviously not," Johnny sneered.

Raine smiled, and the sight was nowhere near pleasant. "Trust me. She's a lot safer with me than you two boobs."

And he just called the lawmen boobs? Mariana had the insane urge to laugh, so she cleared her throat. The only thing she knew about Molotov cocktails was from watching television, but obviously they caused a big fire. What if the person had thrown the bomb inside her house? Maybe she should get out of town, but this guy had found her once, and no doubt he'd do it again.

She did feel safer with Raine at her house. "Nobody knows Raine is here, so this has to be about me. The guy sent more roses today, so he knows where I live and obviously is watching the house." The idea made her want to puke.

The sheriff leaned toward her. "I can take you somewhere safe."

"So can I," Raine said. "She's safe with me, Sheriff. Why don't you go find her stalker?"

The sheriff stared intently. "Where were you when the bomb went off, Mariana?"

"I was sleeping in my bedroom." She chewed on her bottom lip and shivered.

"And you?" The sheriff turned to Raine.

Raine pulled her closer against his side. "I was sleeping in the guest room."

The sheriff looked from one to the other of them. "So it's possible you created this entire situation and Mariana would have no clue. Right?"

"I did not bomb my own truck," Raine spoke slowly.

"Why don't I believe you?" The sheriff shook his head. "Mariana, please trust me. Get away from this man."

She only had a second to go with her gut, and she shook her head. "I'm fine. He isn't the stalker." God, she hoped her instincts were on track this time.

What if she was wrong?

Chapter 8

The anger rushing through Raine's veins actually burned. This stalker, whoever he was, had dared to bomb the truck with Mariana very close inside the house. Oh, Raine had planned to find the guy, teach him a lesson, and then turn him over to the law. Now he just wanted to cut off the bastard's head.

"I'm sorry about your truck," Mariana murmured, handing him a glass of wine and retaking her seat on the sofa. Now that the sheriff and his imbecile of a son had gone, the atmosphere in the room no longer was filled with tension.

"I don't care about the truck." Raine accepted the drink and downed it in two swallows. Heat splashed through his stomach and down his throat.

She curled one leg beneath her and turned to face him. "I might've put you in danger."

His fingers tingled with the need to sit her on his lap and comfort her. "I'm not worried about danger." The more time he spent with her, the stronger this pull became between them. The branding mark on his palm seared through his skin to bone with insistence. He should've heard or sensed the bomber, even though he'd been asleep. The illness was slowly taking away his abilities, even with Mariana just in the next room. He had to find this guy before he started losing his strength. Mariana could never see him like that.

She reached out and touched his arm. "Are you okay? Any stress can't be good for your condition."

His condition? Oh, for God's sakes. He took her glass, placed it on the coffee table, and lifted her onto his lap. "The last person you need to worry about right now is me."

Her mouth formed a small 'o' and then she settled against him. The scent of her hair, honey and vanilla, wafted up and tempted him. "Why won't you tell me about the possible treatments?" She placed her palm right over his heart.

"You're all I need right now," he murmured, enjoying her touch way too much.

She grinned. "You are so corny."

Since he'd decided not to mate her, he couldn't tell her the whole truth. Unable to stop himself, he leaned down and kissed her. Sweet and gentle, going slow. The woman tasted like peaches, even after drinking the potent wine. God, he fucking loved peaches.

She sighed and leaned against him, tilting her head back to give him better access.

He took the invitation and delved deep, putting everything he couldn't say into the kiss. The longing and the frustration as well as the acceptance and the desire. She got all of him—even if it was only for a few moments. Then he released her mouth. "You should go back to bed. I'll stay out here and keep watch."

"I don't want to go back to bed." She nipped his neck. "Unless you want to come with me."

Hunger slaked him, but he kept his hold loose. "Not a good idea. I hit you with a lot tonight, and then a bomb went off. You don't need to ease my pain, Mariana." Yeah, she was a sweetheart.

She levered back and met his gaze evenly. "I'm not trying to ease you, and I'm not overwhelmed. We've been attracted to each other since our first meeting, you're not my patient, and we both know how short life can be." Her focus dropped to his mouth. "I've never been a game player, and right now, neither one of us has time to play a game. Do you want me or not?"

Considering she was sitting on his rock-hard erection, the question was rather redundant. "You know I do." This could be a colossal mistake. How was he going to touch her—finally touch her—and not mark her for life? For eternity? "You don't know what you're offering." He swept a tendril away from her lovely face.

"I'm offering myself," she whispered, sliding around to face him. To straddle him. "That's all. Just you and me—exploring whatever this is between us for what time we have."

It was more than he'd ever thought he'd get. It was more than he could refuse. For the first time in his long life, he lied to himself. He kissed her again, tasting her sweetness and telling himself that it was just a couple of kisses. He'd stop before they went too far.

The beast of his soul laughed at him, even as it growled in need. There was no 'too far.' Not for him. It wasn't in his nature to hold back, and if he had a sense of honor, he'd let her go right now. Or he'd tell her the full truth—and that was unacceptable. Too soon, he'd be gone, and he would leave her with a knowledge it wasn't safe for her to have. He had to stop this.

But then she scooted even closer, core to core, and dug her hands into his hair. Her kiss was wild, beyond anything he'd ever experienced. Her tongue slid into his mouth, past the fangs that wanted so badly to descend, right into him.

He growled, low and with a craving that was rapidly taking control. The feeling of her tight little body on him shot right to his balls, lighting a path of fire on the way. He forgot about honor and forgot about protecting her for her own safety.

There was only right now and this female on him. The need to get inside her, to become complete for the first time in his life, propelled him to grasp her hips and hold her in place. Her wild movements and her merciless curves were going to kill him.

He could hear the blood rushing through her veins, and an unbearable thirst slaked through him. Would her blood taste like peaches? Could he bite her…just enough to taste?

The female had no idea how close she was to becoming his. Forever. His fangs started to drop on their own, and he wrenched his mouth free, licking along her jawline to the pounding pulse in her neck.

He nipped hard enough to make her jump and then stood, lifting her. "Are you sure?"

"Yes," she breathed, wrapping her arms around his neck and biting lightly.

The immortal inside him roared with hunger.

* * * *

Mariana had lost her mind but she didn't care. Not one bit. The man carrying her into her bedroom was strong and wild, and she wanted more. She wanted all of him. She licked beneath his jaw and then nipped as hard as he had. God, he was delicious. Every movement of muscle against her only made her crave everything he could give her.

He set her on the bed and used his thumbs to slide her sweater up and over her head. Then he pulled her closer into a blood-stirring kiss, turning even her bones to mush. Her lungs seized, and she breathed him in. Then he pulled her sports bra over her head, baring her breasts.

"God, you're beautiful," he murmured, gently tracing each breast and scraping the pads of his thumbs across her nipples.

Electricity zagged from his touch to her core. She moaned and reached for his zipper.

"Not yet." He leaned down and pulled her jeans down her legs, his talented thumbs caressing her skin on the way. Her panties came next, and then she was completely nude. His wide palms spread across her thighs, and then he dipped his head, kissing her right on the sex.

Her legs trembled. "Raine." Every inch of her was hypersensitive and ready for him. Just for him.

He chuckled and slid his fingers into the wetness of her sex. She sucked in a breath and opened wider for him, her body rioting with a need so great she couldn't think. When he took his touch away, she swore.

His chuckle was a dangerous tease.

"I don't want slow this first time," she ground out, levering up on her elbows. "Later."

"Hmmm." He leaned down again and kissed her, this time running his tongue between her folds. He found the aching bundle of nerves and sucked. Hard.

She cried out at the searing pleasure and bucked against him. His strong hands went to her hips, and he held her to the bed, licking and sucking without mercy. Without giving her time to breathe, his wicked mouth drove her so high she could only fall over the cliff. She cried out, the orgasm rippling through her with a sharp edge she could barely ride.

Sighing, she came down, even as her body was still on fire. For him. "Raine."

"Yeah." He stood and shucked his pants, leaving his exquisite body on full display. A tattoo wound over his right arm, crested with an M with a bunch of spikes—much like the one on his hand but not quite as brutal looking. "You taste delicious, and we're going to do that again tonight. A couple of times." He moved up her body, his skin touching hers and his masculine scent surrounding her.

She tunneled her hands through his hair, pulling the thick waves away from his face. Oh, she liked this face. She liked him. Maybe more than like, but that didn't make sense. How could he be dying?

"None of that." He took her mouth, pulling her out of her sad thoughts and right into desperate passion. One wicked hand moved down her body and stroked her—demanding this time and not gentle. "You're ready."

God, she was ready. "Yes," she said against his mouth, her nipples hard against his even harder chest.

He positioned himself between her thighs and pressed his thick head at her opening.

Desire rushed through her, different than ever before. She held her breath, wanting something. Wanting him. Needing him.

He kissed her again while pushing inside her, stretching her tight. Oh, there was so much of him. She held on, her heart beating wildly in her chest. Slowly, he kept pushing, not stopping. Taking her. Definitely taking her. Finally, he drove the last couple of inches right to the hilt.

She arched at the overwhelming sense of him. Of invasion and of something else. Something that felt complete and whole. He pulled out only to power back inside her, setting up a slow and steady pace that had her fingers digging into his scalp.

"You feel so good," he ground out, his unreal green gaze capturing hers.

He felt amazing. "Please don't stop," she whispered, her internal walls clamping down on him as if she'd never let him go.

"I promise." He drove harder, deeper, more.

She came close to shattering several times, and the second she caught her breath, he paused or slowed down, keeping her on the edge. They rode that fine line, sweat dotting her forehead, her thoughts incoherent. Finally, she released his head and dug her nails into his chest. "Now, Raine. Now."

"Now," he whispered, hammering into her with fierce power.

She clamped her legs to his thighs and spiraled into a climax so wild she could only open her mouth silently. The orgasm shattered her, taking her thoughts and leaving a blinding pleasure behind.

He followed a second later on a rough groan, his body jerking against her. His head dropped to her neck, and he scraped his teeth along her jugular.

She caught her breath and turned her head instinctively, giving him better access.

He stilled and then gently kissed her. "Oh, baby. You have no idea," he murmured, nipping her earlobe.

She caressed down his sides, so content she wanted to purr. That was the most incredible sex ever created. She opened her eyes just as he lifted his head. For the briefest of seconds, his eyes looked like a pure silver. She blinked and then squinted. Nope. Green. A startling green, but definitely green. She grinned. "I think that blew my mind." Now she was even seeing things.

"Just wait," he said, kissing her nose.

She laughed. "I like that you're close to your Grams."

"Me, too," he said. "She's a spitfire and reminds me of you."

Now that was the sweetest thing. "I get that from my mom. She's a journalist right now in South Korea working on a story." She'd like Raine quite a lot, actually.

"What about your father?" Raine ran a lazy hand down her arm.

She shrugged. "He left my mom when I was young and created another family. I know him but we're not close. It's my mom and me, and I had a great childhood and played tons of sports. Mom often coached whatever sport I was playing at the time. Then I went to college on a golf scholarship, which was pretty cool."

"I like that about you." He kissed her forehead.

She smiled and then blinked as she realized he was hardening inside her already. Wow. Just wow. "Are you a machine or what?" she murmured, her body perking up for another round.

"Or what," he confirmed, his mouth already on hers.

Chapter 9

Raine stared at the burned-out carcass of his truck. The silver paint had bubbled into black blobs, the interior was crusty, and the windows were all shattered.

"It's totaled," Evan muttered, crouching down to peer beneath the sidewall.

Raine looked at the demolished engine compartment. "Yep." He measured the distance from the truck to the front door. "The guy could've just as easily thrown the projectiles through the front window." The thought that Mariana had been that close to danger the night before tightened the muscles in his neck until his head ached.

"This stalker has upped his game." Evan peered into what used to be the back seat. "There was no hint of violence in the Dallas records." He paused and turned toward Raine. "This is directed at you, but if he's obsessed with Mariana, he's going to see your new, ah, friendship as a betrayal."

Friendship. Well, that was one way to put it. The sounds of her sighs from the night before were still running through his head, and he wanted more. A lot more. "I'm aware," Raine said, ignoring the smoke still wafting from the engine area.

Evan dusted soot off his hands and stood to his full height. He'd filled out quite a bit since mating Tabi, although he'd been a big guy as a human. Well, he was still human but now had extra chromosomal pairs making him immortal. "I'm new to this world of yours."

"I know," Raine said, studying a male he now considered a friend. "How are you doing?"

Evan shrugged. "Fine, I guess. All of the secrecy and uncertainty is a pain, however. There aren't any human males who've mated immortals that we can find. I'm sure they're out there, but apparently I have to stay under the radar, so I don't know what to expect."

"None of us know with you," Raine admitted. "So long as you're not nuts and trying to take out whole cities, I figure you're fine."

"I don't want to hurt anybody," Evan said, looking like the cop he'd been for so long. "This new strength is taking some time to get used to, and I have to stop accidentally breaking cell phones or I'm going to run out of money. My senses are strong, too. I can smell Mariana all over you."

Raine tilted his head. Was Evan going to warn him off in an effort to protect the fragile shrink? "Your point?"

The cop shrugged, looking around the quiet neighborhood. "If you're immortal, why can't you mate her? She obviously likes you, and immortality ain't bad."

Raine didn't have time for this. "I already explained enough. My time is limited."

Evan met his gaze directly, and a dark blue rim surrounded his normally blue iris. That was new. "Immortals don't get sick, as far as I understand. So how is your time limited? You really are going to have to explain that."

"I really don't," Raine said mildly, acutely aware of the oath he'd taken at the age of ten to protect his family. His reaching out to Faith Cooper was as close to breaking that vow as he'd ever come, and he wasn't going to change that with this new immortal. "Just promise that when I'm gone, you'll look out for Mariana."

"Of course," Evan said easily. "Tabi really likes her. I'm sure we'll be able to find her a nice immortal to mate so she can live forever. My demoness seems to be a bit of a matchmaker, if you ask me."

Raine rolled his eyes. "Nice try." The thought of Mariana mating somebody else was like a kick in the balls, but he wasn't going to play that game with Evan. He stretched his neck and looked toward the quiet home. After going all night with the stunning brunette, he should be tired, but instead he felt invigorated. Healthy again.

She had that effect on him.

Shit. She was *supposed* to have that effect on him.

Movement sounded, and two police cars zoomed down the street, screeching to a stop. The sheriff leaped out of his with his gun out. "Put your hands up. Now."

Raine looked at Evan and then back at the sheriff while the other officer opened her door and held her gun pointed at him. "What the hell?"

Evan frowned at his former boss. "What in the world are you doing?"

The sheriff ignored him. Today he'd dressed in a nicely pressed uniform, and his hair was groomed. He still had the slight beer belly going on, though. "Turn and put your hands on the vehicle, Maxwell."

Raine sighed. "I don't have time for this shit, buddy. What's going on?"

Evan stepped toward the sheriff. "Baker—this is a bad idea."

"Shut up or I'll arrest you, too," the sheriff snapped. "Marlene. Now."

The blonde female officer strode around her car door, her gaze apologetic. "Turn around, Mr. Maxwell."

Mariana and Tabi walked out onto the porch.

"What's going on?" Mariana asked.

Raine stiffened. "False arrest, apparently." He could take care of the sheriff in a heartbeat, but the curvy blonde officer was just doing her job. He cut a look at Evan.

Evan nodded. "I'll take care of things here. Is there a lawyer you want me to call?"

"Yeah. Hit speed dial 3 on my phone. It's inside." Raine turned and allowed the officer to cuff him and lead him to her car. He looked over the top of it. "Mariana? Stay inside and safe until I get out and begin legal proceedings against this dumbass sheriff." Then he sat in the backseat, his temper at bay since Evan had promised to stay and look after Mariana along with Tabi. Although the way the demoness was staring at the sheriff, she might go for the brain attack. At this point, Raine didn't care.

The last thing he saw before the car sped away was Mariana's pale face.

* * * *

This was unbelievable. Mariana stormed into her house and reached for Raine's phone on the counter to speed dial # 3.

"Yo, bro. You get the deed done?" A male voice came over the line—one with a similar deep timbre to Raine.

"Um, this is Mariana Lopez and Raine Maxwell said to call this number?"

Quiet came across for a second. "Is Raine all right?"

"Healthy, yes. But he was just arrested and said to call you. Are you his lawyer?" She bit her lip.

"If he needs a lawyer, then I'm his lawyer," the guy said. "Mariana, huh?"

She turned as Evan shut the front door and Tabi looked at her expectantly. "Yes."

"Good. I'm actually, uh, close by and will take care of this." The guy disengaged the call.

Mariana pulled the phone from her ear to stare at it. "Weird. Definitely weird."

The door opened, and the sheriff walked inside.

"Get out of my house," Mariana burst out, moving right for him. Her body was still tingling from the night she'd shared with Raine, and there was no way he should've been arrested.

Tabi stopped her by the arm. "Hold on. Let me kick him out. I haven't had any fun lately." The miniature blonde rocked back on her heels as if ready for a good fight.

Mariana paused. Oh, Tabi was tough, but she was half the size of the sheriff. "I can handle this."

"I've got it." Evan yanked the door open wider and reached for the sheriff.

"Wait," Mariana ordered. "If you touch him, he'll press charges. However, since he's trespassing in my house—"

"Enough," the sheriff grumbled, his eyes blazing. It was odd that both he and Raine had green eyes, but the greens couldn't be any different. Raine's eyes were a deep and true green, while the sheriff's were slightly muddy and cloudy.

Mariana held up a hand. "Sheriff—"

"Buck Baker. Please call me Buck. Please." The sheriff tapped a manilla file folder against one hand. "Tell your friends to leave and let me help you."

"Not a chance in hell," Tabi said, her voice sweet and her eyes glowering.

The sheriff looked down at the file folder. "You need to see this."

Mariana frowned. "What is it?"

He moved into the living room and sat on the sofa.

Mariana steeled her shoulders and walked into her living room, choosing the seat across the coffee table. Tabi sat in the other chair while Evan remained standing like a guard at post. "What's in the folder?"

The sheriff set the papers on the table and flipped the folder around with one finger. "Raine Maxwell has been stalking you since you were in Dallas."

She looked down at the top flap. "That's impossible." Her neck—and her thighs—were both whisker burned from the man.

"Okay." The sheriff opened the file folder to show a picture of Raine sitting on a park bench with a blue ball cap over his thick hair. He had a latte in one hand and his phone in the other, and he looked relaxed.

A lump rose in Mariana's throat. "That's across from my old clinic in Dallas." Her ears started to ring. This couldn't be happening.

The sheriff slid the photo out of the way to show two more, one at her dry cleaners with her in the front of the line and the other when she was out with friends at a steak restaurant. There he sat at the bar, out of her line of sight but clearly keeping her within his. "I can't breathe." She shoved the pictures away.

Tabi took them, looking each over. "Where did you get these, Sheriff?"

"The Dallas police sent copies of all surveillance they've captured in the case, and as you can tell, Raine is difficult to make out as the same guy in each one. Mariana, you probably looked at some of the videos and didn't recognize him."

"Because I hadn't met him yet," she said slowly. "Not until he showed up at the anger management group."

The sheriff winced and tugged out another piece of paper from the bottom of the pile showing 'no records found.' "Speaking of which, I went through all of our recent court records, and he wasn't arrested or sent to anger management by a judge. Whatever documentation he gave to you was falsified."

Evan leaned closer to peer at the photos. "Is that normal?" He seemed to be asking Tabi.

"Of course not," Mariana burst out. "That's creepy and stalkerish."

Tabi nodded. "I agree. That is not normal behavior. For anybody."

Mariana held a hand to her trembling mouth. Raine had watched her in Dallas, and here he was now in Indiana. She'd trusted him. Heck. She'd slept with him. "How can it be him?" she whispered.

The sheriff leaned over and patted her hand with his smooth one.

"These guys are really good at what they do. Anybody would've fallen for his charm."

Fallen for his charm? She'd fallen right into his bed. Her heart hurt worse than her head right now, and there was a migraine on its way. "These pictures aren't enough to show a stalking case, right? I mean, we have to prove he sent the flowers."

"And bombed his own truck?" Tabi asked, setting down the pictures. "That doesn't make any sense. Why would he ruin his truck?"

The sheriff spared her a glance. "Obviously to throw us off his tail as well as make Mariana feel vulnerable and in need of protection, which he was more than happy to provide."

He'd provided more than that. Multiple orgasms to be exact. Mariana clenched her teeth together. "I feel sick." He'd seemed so genuine and kind. "What about this disease he has? Is that false, too?" Her head was telling her to look at the evidence, but her heart was still fighting the reality. Those pictures were real and did not lie.

The sheriff snorted. "He has a disease?"

"A degenerative one," Mariana said slowly.

"Yeah. He looks sick," the sheriff muttered. "Not. Unbelievable."

Mariana rubbed her hands down her jeans. "I did wonder how the guy found me here. If Raine was the stalker in Dallas, he must've followed me." But it didn't feel right. Not after the night they'd shared.

The sheriff patted her hand again. "I'm glad we arrested him."

Tabi lifted her head. "Arrested him? Like booked him?"

"Yes." The sheriff sat taller. "I'm sure he's being fingerprinted right now."

Tabi looked at Evan. "Crap. This is worse than we thought."

Chapter 10

The only thing that kept Raine from losing his damn mind was the fact that Evan and Tabi were with Mariana. He sat in a cell for nearly an hour before the sheriff deigned to take him to an interrogation room. The human's satisfied smile nearly got him punched in the mouth.

Apparently Raine's thoughts showed on his face because the sheriff lost the smile and hustled them to the room, securing his cuffs to a bar across the table.

Then he sat across from him. "Sorry about the delay but I was running through the case with Mariana." The possessive tone and purposeful use of the woman's first name set Raine's teeth on edge.

Yet he kept his bored façade in place. "Lawyer. Want one. Now."

The sheriff sighed. "Now Raine. Is that really necessary? Don't you want to get this taken care of? I think in your own sick way, you care for Dr. Lopez. How about you tell me everything, and I figure out a way to help you here? I think you need help."

Raine studied the man. His eyes had dilated when he'd said Mariana's name. "You're interested in her."

The sheriff's eyebrows lifted. "This is a case." His eyes darted left and then back.

"You know, you're not a very good liar." Raine crossed his arms.

The door opened, and his brother strode in, briefcase in hand.

Raine looked him up and down. "What the fuck?"

Cade kept his serious expression in place. "I was close by."

Raine's nostrils flared as the reality hit him square center. "Were you, now?"

Cade had the decency to wince. "We thought it was a good idea."

Oh, Raine was going to throw him through the door face first. "Who was with you?" Already he knew. Of course he knew. Cade and Collin were twins and rarely did stupid stuff alone.

"Collin," Cade admitted. "We didn't hurt anybody, and it seemed like a good idea at the time."

The sheriff cleared his throat. "What the hell are you two talking about?"

"Nothing," Raine growled. "It's a family matter that we'll talk about later." With a punch or two to the face. The twins had kidnapped him and Mariana to force his hand. He might have to kill them.

Cade relaxed. "Yes. Family matter to handle later. Right now, let's deal with this."

Raine looked him over. "Nice suit." It was gray and probably cost more than ten grand. When his brother played a part, he did it with style.

"This old thing?" Cade drawled.

The sheriff stood and puffed out his chest before holding out a hand. "Sheriff Baker."

"Cade Maxwell." Cade must've gripped too tightly when they shook, because the sheriff failed to hide his wince. "I'm Raine's brother as well as his attorney. Well, one of his many attorneys. We do like to sue people."

Raine cut him a look. Cade was twenty years younger at almost three hundred and eighty years old and was just as broad across the chest and as tall as Raine, but his hair was a burnished brown and his eyes a cerulean blue. "Get me out of here."

"Not happening." The sheriff retook his seat.

Cade strode around to sit next to Raine. "All right, Sheriff. Show me what you've got."

The sheriff then proceeded to show them pictures of Raine in Dallas as well as the records search showing that Raine was never sentenced to anything in Indiana.

Cade leaned forward. "Well. This is a disaster." He rubbed his smooth shaven chin. While Raine's face was all hard angles, Cade had more of a rugged and square look to him. "I mean, it's horrible."

The sheriff smiled and looked at Cade with respect in his eyes. "Exactly. Help me to help your brother. The guy is sick."

Raine sat back to watch. Why not?

Cade blinked. Once. Just once. "Why, Sheriff, I was talking about your case. I mean, come on. You have pictures of my client in Dallas, and none of them show Dr. Mariana Lopez in them. Well, except for this one in the bar. As you can tell, Raine is sitting next to what can only be considered a stunning redhead in a dress that was truly lovely, even if a size too small. He was on a date."

The sheriff scoffed. "On a date at the same bar and restaurant Mariana was having dinner at with friends? On the same night?"

"It's a hot spot for young couples," Cade returned.

"Ha," the sheriff muttered. "Mariana would never fall for that line of bullshit."

Cade cut Raine a look. "Mariana? The sheriff seems to have a familiarity with the woman here. Please tell me this is a jealous male situation. I always get such a good payment from juries for those."

"No." The sheriff slammed his hand on the table. "Dr. Lopez is a citizen in my town, and I'm concerned for her safety. The bomb your client threw into his own truck could've started her home on fire. This is dangerous, Mr. Maxwell. I know you have a job to do, but think of the bigger picture."

Cade smiled, and it was a clear warning. "You really believe my client blew up his own truck? He loved that truck. Trust me. A jury will be crying for him when I'm done talking about that truck and how he willingly let it burn to make sure *Mariana* was protected in the house."

"Raine has been sending her white roses. She hates those," the sheriff barked, his eyes darkening and his complexion turning ruddy.

Raine could almost feel sorry for him. Almost.

"I assume you have proof of that slanderous allegation?" Cade asked.

The sheriff's nostrils flared, but he didn't speak.

"That's what I thought," Cade said. "I do hope you haven't kept my client here for hours based on a hunch, Sheriff. Not only does that kind of thing get a city sued, it usually results in the removal of the authority who made such a fucked-up mistake."

The sheriff leaned forward. "Oh yeah? What about the order that forced your brother into Dr. Lopez's anger management group? He showed her documentation, and there isn't any."

"Do you have a copy of said documentation?" Cade asked.

"No, but Mariana confirms that she saw it." Now the sheriff smiled. "She'll make a great witness, don't you think?"

Irritation flushed through Raine, and he started to sit straighter, but Cade waved him down.

"It is a pity somebody played such a terrible joke on my brother by sending the order to him in the mail. He had gotten into a bit of a brawl a few weeks before, and he figured the group session was in leu of going to court - at least that's what the document said." Cade sighed and shook his head sadly. "He didn't call me."

"Bullshit," the sheriff snapped.

"Sheriff, I understand your emotions are at play here since you're interested in Dr. Lopez, but we really must stick to the facts. Raine did receive that document in the mail, and it's long gone. I'm sure he threw it away after graduating from the class," Cade said.

Raine dutifully nodded, even though the prickle at the base of his neck was starting to really irritate him. "I want out of here. Now." He had to get back to Mariana.

A deputy opened the door and handed over a series of papers to the sheriff. "We ran him and there's no record. He's clean."

Tension rolled from his brother. Raine inwardly groaned. He'd figured they'd have time to stop his prints from being put into the system, but apparently the sheriff had been determined. Shit. He glanced at his brother.

The look he got back wasn't reassuring.

He sighed again.

* * * *

Lightning zinged outside in proportion to her current mood. Mariana shoved clothing into a bag, her head pounding and her stomach cramping. "I can't believe this."

Tabi stood in the doorway, watching her with worried eyes. "I'm sure there's a reasonable explanation."

"Like what?" Mariana carefully chose which socks she wanted to take.

"I'm not sure," Tabi admitted.

Mariana zipped the bag and pulled it into the living room. "There isn't enough evidence to hold Raine, and you know it."

Evan still stood by the front door. "I think we should at least let him explain. If there's no good explanation, we can keep you safe, Mariana." The ex-cop's eyes blazed a fierce promise, but even he looked uncertain.

There was something Mariana was missing, and she couldn't figure out what. "I can keep myself safe." She tucked her gun into her purse. "For now, I just need some space to figure all of this out." She'd already called Laura in Dallas with the updates, and she was running a background check on Raine Maxwell right now.

"I'll come with you," Tabi offered.

Mariana smiled at her new friend. "You're just rebuilding your factory, and Evan is in the middle of a campaign for sheriff. You don't have time to hide out with me." Tabi's factory, which built some kind of ski masks, had mysteriously blown up earlier that year.

"Friends are more important than any of that," Tabi said, looking so petite next to Evan's large form.

Mariana shook her head. She could take care of herself, but she wasn't sure she could protect Tabi at the same time. "I'm not going away for good." She'd wait to hear from Laura about Raine's background and then come up with a plan. The local sheriff would help her, and if Evan was elected, he would as well—just in case Raine was a crazy stalker.

How could the man who'd given her the best night of her life be her stalker? It just didn't make sense.

Worse yet, maybe it made perfect sense. If he had been stalking her, she'd given him exactly what he'd wanted. Her. "I'm so confused," she admitted.

"Then wait and talk to him," Evan advised, the gun at his hip looking like it lived there.

She shook her head. "You don't understand. When I'm around him, I believe him. He's charming and smart, and we slept together." She might as well tell them the full truth. "I need time and distance from him to be able to think this through."

"I get that," Tabi said. "But you shouldn't go alone."

"I'm not alone. I have my gun, and you two are just a phone call away." She grabbed her keys off the table and headed toward the garage. "I'll let you know where I land when I get there." She had a spa in mind—she'd been looking at the place for a while. A couple of massages, a lot of champagne, and some quiet time was just what she needed. "Don't worry."

"Where are you going?" Evan asked.

Temptation to tell him warred with the lessons in survival she'd learned the last year. "I'll decide on the road, and I promise I'll call when I get there." She'd let Laura in Dallas know where she ended up. "I'll miss you two." Then she jogged out to her car, opened the garage door, and drove off like she knew what she was doing.

She had no clue what she was doing. Except escaping for now.

Sometimes that had to be enough. She called Laura. "I'm on the road. Any news?"

"Not yet, but we're doing a deep dive on the guy. Are you going to that spa?" Laura asked.

"Yeah. I'll call you when I check in and am safe. Thanks, Laura." She clicked off the call, keeping it short. Oh, she seriously doubted Raine had the ability to trace her calls, but just in case, she was going to be careful. If Raine was the stalker. What if he wasn't and somehow he had an explanation for all of this? Just in case, she kept an eye on her rearview mirror and surroundings, making sure she wasn't followed.

The luxury spa hotel was about three hours away, and she finally started to relax after the second hour. Rain pelted down in an impressive autumn storm, but she kept a slow and steady pace. She pulled off the interstate at a rest stop, parked right up front, locked her car, and took her purse with gun inside. After taking care of business, she walked outside, feeling better than she had all day.

Her car was gone.

She paused. Wait a minute. She'd parked right up front. Shit. The place was fairly empty save for a luxury SUV parked down the way. Turning to run, she tried to grab for her gun. Strong arms yanked her back, and something covered her face.

Her scream came out muffled, and then confusion slid through her veins. She tried to push the cloth away, but her arms were too heavy to move.

Then, nothing. She fell into unconsciousness with one more gasp of tainted breath.

Chapter 11

The growl of thunder jerked Mariana awake. Her head ached, and her mouth felt like it was stuffed full of cotton. She swallowed several times and tried to stretch her heavy limbs. Was she in bed? What was happening?

The chilly ground permeated her jeans and light jacket. Reality threw her into awakening fully. She sat up and then gasped as her head swam. Ouch. Okay. She blinked her eyes open to find herself in a small closet with shelves containing cleaning supplies. The floor was concrete, and the shelves plastic wire. The lone door was across from her, and somebody had left the light on.

Memories from the rest stop floundered through her head. A man had grabbed her. Who was it. Was it Raine? A part of her hoped Raine was her kidnapper. At least she knew him.

She gingerly stood and tiptoed to the door to press her ear against it and listen. Nothing. She twisted the knob. Nope. Locked. Bending, she took a good look at it. The thing seemed like a normal lock. Then she looked around at the cleaning supplies. Surely something there could blow the lock or melt it or something. She reached for a bottle of bleach just as the door opened.

Yelping, she jumped back. Then she blinked several times. The man in front of her was taller than Raine, closer to seven feet tall. He was thinner and was wearing some sort of Halloween mask. "Is that mask necessary?"

He motioned her out, and she complied, ready to make a run for it.

"Sit there." He pointed to a metal folding chair next to the closet.

She did so and looked around an empty airplane hangar. Her stomach sank. "Who are you?" Even without the mask, she'd recognize somebody that tall if she already knew him. So this was her stalker, and she had no clue about his real identity.

"You can call me John with no h." He smiled, and the sight was ghoulish. The guy even wore fake teeth? He had long black hair with red tips, and his mask was a pasty and unnatural white color with blue veins. His contacts turned his eyes a freaky purple, and his teeth were yellowed and too sharp looking. "You're Mariana."

"I am," she said, eyeing the door to the far right. The hangar door was shut, but she could make it to the human-sized door in a few seconds.

"Don't make me tie you up. It seems so unnecessary." Jon's voice was gritty but not too hoarse.

She took a deep breath and tried not to hyperventilate. Panicking wasn't going to help her out of this. For some reason, her stalker didn't want her to see his face. That was good, right? He wouldn't kill her if she couldn't identify him. For now, she had to use her knowledge as a psychologist and figure out who he was without angering him. "What did you think when we first met?"

He frowned, and darn if the mask didn't move perfectly with his face. "Huh?"

Okay. He must really be in a delusional state. "Why are we here, Jon?" That was an innocuous statement.

He frowned and studied her as if she was missing brain cells. "We're waiting for transport to headquarters. The plane is on its way, but the storm is hampering its travel. We might be here for several hours."

Headquarters? "I don't want to go to your spaceship," she snapped, letting fear take over common sense.

He smiled, flashing those sharp canines again. "Stop playing dumb. You know you're enhanced. What do you comprehend of the Kurjan people?"

Okay. This guy was beyond delusional. The outside door opened, and two more men wearing masks walked inside. Like Jon, they had on plain black pants and shirts. They paused and flanked the doorway, gazes flicking to her. They also wore the black and red wigs and the too pale masks.

Was this some kind of a cult?

"What's up with the masks?" she asked.

Jon crouched next to her, still taller than she. His contacts had some red mingling with the purple. "You're enhanced and you've created a marking already. Surely you know about us."

It was like he spoke another language. "I have no idea," she whispered. The guy smelled like too sweet musk.

He frowned, and the mask wrinkled perfectly. "Interesting. You've never heard of us?"

She shook her head. So far, he'd seemed rather approachable.

"Have you heard of species other than humans? Surely you have." He placed a large and bony hand on her knee.

She barely kept from jumping away from his touch. His hand felt cold through her jeans. Other species? "Like animals?"

"No." He chuckled. "Like Kurjans, vampires, demons, and so on. Well, I guess shifters are animals, but we don't intermingle with them much."

She tried to swallow over her dry throat. Were they going to drain her blood? "You think you're a vampire?"

"Of course not." His smile slid away from his blood-red lips. "I'm a Kurjan."

"Oh." She could play along a little, but she needed information. Were the white roses part of their ritual? "How long have you been stalking me, Jon?"

"Stalking? I just got the orders to take you this morning. Our techs narrowed down your location, and we followed you from your home today. Thank you for making it so easy." He patted her knee.

"I didn't see you following me." She pushed his hand away.

He nodded. "We're good at the job."

She shook her head as the fear rose in her until it was difficult to breathe. "You're talking in riddles. Did you or did you not send me the white roses?"

"I don't send roses." He leaned in to examine her eyes and ignored the fact that she shrank back. "Did I give you too much chloroform? Sometimes I get it wrong."

"Please stop playing games." There had to be a way to reason with him. "It sounds like somebody else ordered you to kidnap me." If so, who the hell was her stalker? "Was it Raine?"

"Never heard of Raine," Jon said. "Our techs found you based on a report filed in Dallas that mentioned a probable stalker with a mating marking on his hand."

"Mating marking?" The only person she knew with a tattoo on his hand was Raine.

"Yeah. I'm sure the nerds caught wind of a marking and traced it back to you." He leaned in to sniff her. "It hasn't been transferred yet, so you're free game. We've been collecting enhanced females for a while."

She didn't like the idea of being collected. "Stop this. Now. Take off the mask." Her voice trembled but she faced him directly.

He sighed and leaned toward her. "You take it off."

Fine. She grabbed his neck and searched for the mask. Nope. Was it a whole body suit? Glaring at him, she pulled on his wig. The hair remained in place, and he winced. That was his real hair? She felt along his hairline for the mask. Nothing.

He smiled again. "See? It's all me." Then fangs slowly lowered from his mouth.

She screamed.

* * * *

Raine nearly lost his mind when he reached Mariana's and discovered she was gone. A quick call to Tabi confirmed that she'd headed out and hadn't told anybody where. He ran to his brother's rented car and jumped in. "Let's go."

Only Cade would find a new Camaro to rent in the middle of Indiana. He gunned it. "Where are we going?"

Raine pulled his phone out of the bag supplied by the cops when he'd been released. "I put a tracker in her purse. Head to the Interstate and go north."

Cade laughed and sped up. "Of course you did."

Raine dug into the computer tracker he'd placed on her phone to see she'd made a reservation at a spa retreat three hours to the north. His shoulders slowly unbound. Okay. If she was at a spa, she was safe. "Just hurry up," he muttered.

Cade shook his head. "Do you want to explain to me why we're speeding after your wayward mate?" He took a corner on two wheels and sped up onto the Interstate. "This is like a lot of trouble for a female you have no intention of making yours."

"She's in danger," Raine gritted out.

Cade passed three cars on the right. "It seems as if she has taken precautions to keep herself safe. If you're not making her yours, perhaps you should leave her alone."

"No." Raine checked the app on his phone to see the route she'd taken. She'd stopped at what appeared to be a rest stop, and then she'd taken a detour in the wrong direction of the spa. Was she just being careful or had something gone wrong?

Everything in his gut told him she'd had no intention of going east. He quickly dialed Benny again, putting him on speaker this time.

"What, dude? I'm in the middle of trying to rescue my mate, who doesn't know she's my mate, and I need to get kidnapped and have the crap beat out of me each time in order to just find her fucking location. I don't have the energy to deal with you," Benny grumbled. "Make this quick."

There was too much to unpack in that statement. "I'm sorry. Don't you have a hacker in your merry band of misfits? Somebody who can break into traffic or surveillance cameras?" Raine asked.

"Of course, and she's right here in the computer room trying to find my next place of being kidnapped. You can borrow her for three seconds. Raine, this is Mercy. She's a Fae and is just as crazy-assed as rumored to be, so ask her for a favor and then prepare yourself to someday pay up. Mercy? This is my buddy, Raine. He helped Ivar out not too long ago."

"Yeppers?" A soft female voice came over the line.

"Hi. I need a favor and am happy owing you one," Raine said.

The woman chuckled. "Any friend of Benny and Ivar's is somebody who'd I'd like to owe me a favor. What do you need?"

Raine rattled off the time and place of the rest stop. "I need to know what happened to my woman there." He waited.

His brother glanced at him but wisely didn't say anything.

"Okie doke." Rapid typing came over the line. "There is a CCTV camera at the rest stop, and somebody is in the process of wiping it…right now." Her voice rose, and the speed of the typing came faster. "All right. It's going quickly. A woman meeting that description was taken by…holy crap it's a Kurjan in daylight. Well, there's rain and a storm, but they really can go into daylight now."

It was a new development for their species and one Raine didn't have time to ruminate on right now. "Was she hurt?" he growled.

Mercy stopped typing. "The video is gone. It looked like he drugged her and carried her off. I can't see where they went, but I can start looking for traffic cameras."

"No you can't," Benny argued in the background. "You're working on my project."

"It's okay," Raine said. "I have a tracker on her and they obviously took her purse with them. I've got a bead on her."

Benny sighed loudly. Very loudly. "Do you need backup? I could fly there."

"No. My brother is with me," Raine said. "Good luck on your next mission, and Mercy, I owe you one."

"Yes, you do." The female ended the call.

Raine flipped back to the app. "Mariana is stationary at a small and private airport." Then he looked at the raging storm outside. "Hopefully they won't try to fly in this."

Cade passed two logging trucks, and they were just a blur. "How did the Kurjans find her?"

Raine's chest ached with a fire that burned beyond his body. "I have no idea. Hurry up. We're running out of time."

Chapter 12

Mariana couldn't breathe. Was she drugged? She had to be on drugs. There's no way that guy's face was real. Kurjans, vampires, and shifters? Also demons? This was too weird. What was that about the marking on Raine's hand that they'd been talking about? None of it was making sense. This had to be a cult, and she had to be seriously drugged right now. "What did you give me?"

Jon shook his head. "You should be okay now. Take a deep breath."

A monster was telling her to go Zen? This was ridiculous. The only explanation besides a drugging was that he'd had his face surgically changed. Her legs started to tremble. It was a good thing she was sitting. "All right. Say I believe you, and I'm not sure I do, what's the plan here? Why have you kidnapped me?"

"Smart question," Jon said, his eyes more amethyst than reddish-purple now. "I was starting to doubt your intelligence. I'll explain this to you as if you didn't know any of it, which is often possible, except you've brought out an immortal's mating mark, so I think you might be playing a game." He didn't sound too put out by the idea, though.

She shook her head. If the guys at the door would go back outside, she could kick Jon in the face and run for it. Oh, chances were slim that she'd make it, but it was her only chance. Wait a minute. "Where's my purse?" Her gun was in it.

Jon tilted his head toward a few bags in the corner of the hangar. "It's over there with my equipment, and your weapon is still inside your bag. I'll need to confiscate it, though. Sorry."

"Right." Should she go for the gun or the door? Probably the gun.

"You were saying?"

He stood and stretched his back. Man, he was tall. So were the guys at the door. "There are different species in the world besides humans, but some human females are enhanced with otherworld abilities like physic powers, empathic powers, telekinesis…there are many."

Mariana moved to the edge of her seat. "You're saying I'm psychic?" She wasn't. Not at all.

"No. I'm saying you have an ability beyond human. The most common is empathic powers, and since you're a psychologist, perhaps you felt that deep down in choosing your career." He shrugged as if it didn't matter much.

Yeah, she'd always felt empathic to a small degree but had just figured she was sensitive to others. "So this ability makes me…enhanced?"

"Yes, and enhanced human females can mate an immortal," Jon said casually.

"Mate?" She jumped to her feet. "No. Absolutely not. Not a chance. I am not mating anybody." She sidled away from him.

He pivoted and put his body between her and the corner. "Your agreement isn't necessary but I'm sure would be appreciated. We have a war coming, another one, and we're gathering as many enhanced females as we can before the well is depleted, so to speak. You have a new future. Life is easier if you just embrace it."

Oh, she was going to embrace his face with a bullet. Was he actually believing this stuff?

"We found you because of the 'tattoo' the police in Dallas ran through a database. It's actually a mating mark. We traced it back to you, and here you are."

A mating mark? "Wait a minute. You're saying that Raine's tattoo led you to me? That he's a Kurjan, too?" Was Raine involved with these weirdoes?

"Did he look like a Kurjan? No." Jon's red lips turned down. "Since he has a mating mark, which arose on his skin when he met you, he has demon blood in him somewhere. Oh, he may be mainly another species like witch or vampire, but anybody with demon blood gets the brand. It's supposed to transfer to you during the mating process."

She swallowed. This was insane. "Do you have a mating mark?"

"No. There's no demon blood in me." He grimaced as if the mere thought was distasteful. "When you mate a Kurjan, it'll happen with a bite and sexual relations. No branding. So that should make you happy."

"None of this makes me happy." She turned as if to retake her seat and instead leaped around him and ran as fast as she could toward the corner and her purse.

He snatched her out of the air by her hair, whipping her up. Pain raced along her scalp, and she screamed.

The door burst open, and two male bodies barreled in.

"Mariana!" Raine bellowed.

Relief caught her a second before she plowed her fist as hard as she could into Jon's eye. He yelped and dropped her. She landed on one knee, and pain ricocheted up her leg.

Raine ran toward Jon as the guy at the door started fighting with the two guards.

Jon punched Raine in the face, and Raine punched him back, moving so quickly he was only a blur.

Mariana swung around and pushed to her feet, running for her purse. The sounds of punches, kicks, and grunts filled the space behind her, but she yanked her weapon free and turned around to aim.

Raine took Jon down to the cement floor, whipped a knife out of his boot, and plunged the blade into Jon's neck.

Mariana faltered. Her stomach lurched.

One of the guards tackled Raine from behind and sent them both sprawling across the vacant hangar. They punched and grappled on the cement, fighting for purchase.

The two at the door battled furiously.

Mariana tightened her grip on the gun and tried to point it at one of the Kurjans, but everyone was moving so quickly.

Jon gurgled and reached for the protruding knife handle to yank it out of his neck.

Mariana stepped back. How had he done that? He'd bleed to death now. Yet he sat up, fury dropping those fangs to his lips.

She retreated a yard.

He stood and turned toward her, looking nothing like a human. Slowly, the wound on his neck healed.

She gasped and then stopped breathing. How had he done that? He stepped toward her, and she lifted the gun automatically, firing several times. She hit him dead center in his chest, and he winced but kept moving toward her. She fired again.

Nothing. He didn't even wince this time. The four bullets popped out of his chest and fell onto the cement floor, pinging loudly. "That's impossible," she whispered.

He reached for her, and Raine manacled him around the waist, the momentum propelling them into the solid block wall. The cement crackled from the impact and shards rained down.

Mariana turned to see the Kurjan soldier Raine had fought down on the ground with his head cut off. She gagged. Panic seized her, and she ran toward the door, skirting the battling men and yanking it open. Rain slashed her as she ran outside, desperately looking around the quiet airport.

There were several hangars and one long landing strip all surrounded by forest land. She rushed toward a Camaro parked near the SUV that she'd been kidnapped in and jumped inside, searching wildly for keys. They had to have left the keys. No.

Damn it. She hurried out and ran toward the SUV when the door banged open.

Raine stood there with blood on his face and rips through his dark shirt. His eyes were an unreal green—definitely not human.

It was true. Somehow, it was all true. She took a step back.

He moved toward her with his friend behind him. "We have to go. Now." His voice was grittier than she'd ever heard it.

She shook her head wildly as the rain poured over her face.

He grasped her arm and pushed her into the back of the Camaro before taking the driver's seat and shutting the door. It was only a two-door. She couldn't get out. Just as she scooted to the other side, the passenger door opened, and the other guy got inside. He shut the door.

Raine accepted the keys from the guy and ignited the engine, quickly turning around and driving away from the hangar. "It's still storming, but we have to hurry out of here before their reinforcements arrive." The rain hadn't washed all the blood off his face, and he looked deadly in the rear-view mirror. "Put on your seatbelt, Mariana."

She did so immediately, her mind almost blanking. It was too much. All of it.

The other guy turned. "Hi. I'm Cade." He had light blue eyes, a rugged jaw, and dark hair. The resemblance to Raine was unmistakable. "I'm Raine's much younger brother." His smile would've been charming had he not had a healing hole in his neck and lower jaw.

She shrank back.

Cade sighed. "You really should've told her about us."

Raine kept silent and punched the gas, whipping onto the main road by the small airport. "I had no idea she'd be kidnapped by Kurjans. How the hell had they found her?"

"I'm right here," she snapped, forgetting her terror for a minute. "I told my friend in Dallas about your tattoo and drew it for her. In trying to find my stalker, she conducted a search on the Internet, and—"

Cade groaned. "The Kurjans are monitoring for mating marks. That actually makes sense." He turned and looked at her again. "You're not supposed to share that kind of information, Mariana."

She gaped at him. "Are you fucking kidding me?"

Cade turned to his brother and grinned. "I like her. Lots of spunk. Mom will love her."

Raine zipped onto the Interstate. "Would you just shut up?" He flipped a switch and increased the speed on the windshield wipers. The rain and wind increased in force.

Mariana kicked the back of his chair. "Are you a demon?" She could not even believe she asked that question.

Raine sighed. "Let's talk about it when we get to your place. You're going to need to pack. I'm sorry, but you'll have to move again."

"I'm not going anywhere," she burst out. "Start talking now."

"No." Raine flicked on the lights to battle the storm.

She barely kept from kicking him again. "You are the most stubborn bastard I have ever met."

Cade nodded. "Yep. We all say that."

Mariana turned to him. "Are you a demon?"

Cade grinned. "It sounds like the Kurjans educated you a little bit."

"A lot," she countered. "Although I didn't believe them until Jon pulled the knife out of his neck and healed himself. So it's all true?"

Cade nodded. "It's all true, and we Maxwells do have some demon blood but are mainly vampires. Immortal species usually take on one aspect of their heritage."

Vampires. Oh God. "You're going to kill me and drain my blood." She could feel it draining from her face and head right now.

Cade burst out laughing, and Raine gave her a look in the mirror.

"What?" she asked.

Raine shook his head. "We don't need your blood, we're not going to kill you, and you can't be a vampire. We're just another species, and we're absolutely fine in the sun. We also eat normal food and only take blood during battle or sex."

Battle or sex. Her abdomen did a silly jumpy move it only did around him. Oh, no way. Never again. She crossed her arms over her chest. "You're kidnappers now."

Cade turned toward her and winced. "About that. I should apologize for kidnapping you the other night and taking you to the barn. My twin and I thought that if you and Raine spent some time together that he'd come to his senses. He didn't."

None of this made sense and she didn't care. Wait a minute. "You kidnapped me?"

"Yes. Sorry," Cade said.

It was too much. She kicked the back of Raine's chair again. "I want out of this car."

"No," Raine said.

She growled this time. Actually growled.

Cade laughed out loud again.

Until Raine punched him in the face.

Chapter 13

Raine watched his brother drive off from Mariana's porch while she packed up her belongings. He sent healing cells to his ribs, which he'd ignored since the fight. The sight of the Kurjan soldier grabbing Mariana would haunt him until the end of days. He turned and headed back inside to help her pack.

She sat on the sofa with a glass of red wine and a very set jaw. A stubborn, delicate, firm jaw.

He paused. "I told you to pack."

"I don't give two figs what you told me to do." She took a healthy drink of the dark red brew.

Ah. He rolled his neck to keep his impatience at bay. The woman had been hit with a lot in one day, and she was probably out of sorts. He could be patient. "Listen, Mariana. You've been found by the Kurjans, which means you need to leave here."

She arched one eyebrow in a definite challenge. "I might be new to this crazy world, but they're not regrouping tonight, Raine. You and Cade killed three of them, the tracker you put in my purse is on the side of the Interstate, and I have some time to relax. Maybe not much, but at least I have this night."

It was probably true. "Okay, but you need to go first thing in the morning."

She cocked her head, the movement full of dare.

The blood started rushing faster through his system, and adrenaline poured into his veins.

She took a delicate sip this time. "It's my understanding that if I mate you, the Kurjans will no longer want me."

His cock went rock hard. "We're not mating." His voice lowered to a harsh tone.

"Why not?" She looked at him, her brown eyes luminous in the soft night.

It was a good question. A fair one. "Mariana—"

"Did the mating mark appear on your hand because of me?" She took another drink.

It figured she'd be curious. Who wouldn't be? "Yes."

"When?"

"In Dallas when I was watching you." He crossed around to sit in the chair opposite her.

Her grip visibly tightened on the wine glass. "So you were stalking me in Dallas."

He winced. "Not really." Damn, he would have to explain some of this to her. "There's a coalition of immortal beings called the Realm, and it's powerful and strong. The Maxwells do not belong to it."

Her eyebrows drew down. "Why not?"

It was a risk to tell her their secret, but since he'd gotten her kidnapped by his brothers and then the Kurjans, he'd put her life in danger and owed her that at least. "It depends on who you speak with. The old timers say that we were cursed."

She leaned toward him. "By witches? I heard there are witches."

He grinned. "Witches alter matter by using quantum physics, string theory, and several theories and applications the humans haven't discovered yet. They don't do curses, and they don't ride brooms. They're just another species—a very smart one."

"Oh." She looked at the wine remaining in her glass. "That's interesting. So how could you be cursed?"

He shrugged. "By fate or by science or by whatever. It never mattered. The truth is, now that we know more about genetics, we probably have a genetic mutation that's passed from father to son. Every son gets it, and vampires only make boys, so there you go. We all get it."

She settled back. "That's why you're dying?"

"Yeah," he said softly. "We live to around four hundred years old and then we die."

She sputtered and then sucked in a deep breath. "You're nearly four hundred years old?"

"It's not that old for an immortal," he said, surprised at his defensiveness.

Her mouth gaped open and then shut again. She breathed out. "Most immortals can't die? At all?"

"All immortals can die by beheading and enough fire, although that's rare. The Maxwells usually die from the curse." They should probably find a better name for it, but he did feel cursed, so whatever.

"Why were you following me in Dallas, Raine?" she asked.

He'd thought he'd distracted her from that fact. His grin even felt rueful. "Immortal beings mate for life, and when an immortal mates an enhanced human, usually a woman, she becomes immortal, too. It's an increase in chromosomal pairs. The new immortal might gain some of her mate's abilities, but she usually doesn't get immortal strength or powers."

Mariana looked away as if it was all too much for a moment. "I can't believe this. How have we missed this for so many years?"

"We don't want humans to know. If they knew how possible immortality was, they'd go for it, and there'd be wars. Humans would certainly lose, and in doing so, we'd lose enhanced mates." He kept his voice low and calm.

She shook her head. "I'm not sure I agree."

He needed to tell her the rest of it. "My family usually spends their whole lives trying to find their mates, and more than half the time, they've failed. They die first."

"Why?"

There was the question. The why of it all. "The mutation in our genes. Only our mates can save us." It was as basic as he could make it.

Realization dawned across her angled face. "Mating saves you? Something about the exchange or increase in chromosomes fixes your mutant gene?"

The woman was smart.

"Simply put," he admitted.

She hit him with the next hard question then. "I'm your mate?"

"Yes."

She licked her lips and he wanted to groan. "That's why you were in Dallas?"

"I just wanted to see you." It was hard to explain, and he didn't much understand it himself, except he'd been compelled to see her at least once. Then he had wanted to know everything about her. "We used to search the globe for mates, but now it's much easier. Remember the DNA test you took last year?"

Her mouth dropped open. "Yes. I just wanted to know my heritage."

He nodded. "Our people have tapped into the various databases, and we've gained access to reports. Certain ones point us in certain directions, and we go from there. It was my Grams who actually found you. She's a whiz with computers." Not as good as Cade but close enough.

"So you want to mate me?" Her voice rose a bit with what sounded like panic.

He should be insulted, but he got it. More than she knew. "No. I do not."

* * * *

"What's wrong with me?" Mariana asked the question before she could stop herself and then wanted to smack her forehead the second the words were out.

He grinned and looked almost boyish. Still predatory but close. "Nothing is wrong with you. You're perfect."

Perfect? That was going a bit far. "I don't understand," she whispered.

He reached over and took her hands. "I watched you for four months and fell head over heels. You're perfect, and I can die knowing I found love, even if it was short. Thank you for that."

They were the sweetest words she'd ever heard, and she was well on her way to falling for him, too. Well, she had been before discovering she didn't know much about him. "Wait a minute. Four months?"

A slight red wound beneath his sharp cheekbones. "Yeah." Then he frowned. "During that time, I didn't see another stalker. Oh, I saw the roses arrive at your office and home, but not once did I see somebody else watching you."

That should relieve her, but her entire body felt jittery. This was a lot. More than she'd ever imagined. "Why don't you want to mate me?" Not that she wanted to mate him. Except…he was hot, she liked him, was on the way to loving him, and who wouldn't want to be immortal?

"It's too much of a risk," he said.

She tangled her fingers with his. "Mating is a risk? Do some mates not make it?"

"It is slightly dangerous and can be intense, but the risk isn't in the mating." He sighed. "It's not that easy. Fixing us, making us healthy…it isn't that simple. Those kind of things never are, Mariana."

"Explain." Enough with the half answers.

"Remember when I said that immortal humans don't gain any extra powers?" he asked.

She released his hands and reached for her wineglass. "It was two minutes ago, Raine. Yes, I remember."

"Sarcasm isn't necessary," he drawled. "Unlike most immortals, when a female human mates a Maxwell, both parties get stronger. Freakishly more powerful, especially the immortal. But the female gains strength and abilities that most don't, and that has to be kept a secret from others in order to keep her safe."

She thought about it. "So the danger is in being exposed? So what? You already have that."

"I'm aware," he said. "That's not all."

Of course not. Why would that be all? "Just tell me," she sighed.

"Unlike most matings, the chromosomal exchange in this situation, in *my* situation, creates a relationship based on need. While most immortals don't require the exchange of blood, Maxwells depend on it. If you mated me, we'd have to exchange blood forever. If you wanted to leave me, you couldn't. And part of that, Mariana, is a power you'd give me over you. You'd need me with a desperation you can't even imagine."

She swallowed. Had he meant that to sound sexual? It sounded very sexual. "Sounds like the Maxwell mates have had love and a whole lot of trust in the past."

He shook his head. "Two of my brothers are mated, and it isn't happy or good. Their mates can't stand them, and yet they have to meet up and exchange blood. I think they can work it out, but it's not my business. It can get ugly, Mariana. Very."

She ground a palm into her eye to ward off the headache. "Let me get this straight. My options are to go on the run from the Kurjans because they know I exist. If they find me, they'll probably force me to mate, which sounds horrible." She took a big gulp of her wine, finishing it. "Or I mate you, get a whole slew of new abilities, have to meet up with you every once in a while so we can, what? Bite each other?"

He nodded.

Gross. She looked at the empty wine glass. "In doing so, you'll have a hold on me I might not break free of, if I wanted to. There's a chance I wouldn't want to break free. What's the danger to you, Raine?"

"You could kill me," he said simply.

She sucked in a breath. "Excuse me?"

"If you refused your blood, I'd die. While I might control your body, you'd control my very life."

"I'd never do that," she protested. "Hypothetically to all of this, though."

His smile was tender. "I know. However, if you were captured and kept from me, I'd die. Mating me puts an even bigger bounty on your head than would running from the Kurjans, because we have enemies you can't imagine."

Something in his tone alerted her. "You've seen it happen."

"Yes. More than once. It ended up being torture for both mates, and both eventually died. A horrible death. Our enemies are worse than the Kurjans, and the second I mate you, they're your enemies as well. Your life would be confined to being next to me no matter what, and while you think that's easy, you're far more independent than you realize."

She already knew that. So she'd be giving up this life for one of danger…but it was her choice. "It isn't fair for you to make that choice for me."

He shook his head. "I can keep you safe from the Kurjans and get you a new identity. I can't risk a prolonged and tortuous death for you."

She needed more wine. "Would you risk it for you?"

One of his dark eyebrows rose. "In a heartbeat."

"Then it's my decision, right?" What in the hell was she saying? This was crazy. The entire world had turned upside down in one day. How was it even possible?

"No. It's mine."

There he went again. She leaned toward him. "Do you have fangs?"

"Yes." He let them drop, and they were sharply deadly.

Wow. She watched as he retracted them. "That's incredible. If we mated, would I get fangs?"

He shook his head. "No."

She sat back, her mind reeling. "Wait a minute. Is Tabi an immortal?" The woman had never seemed quite human, actually.

Raine stood. "Tabi is a demoness, and Noah Siosal is a vampire-demon hybrid. Noah mated Abby, and Tabi mated Evan and saved his life. He's an anomaly that we can't expose as well. It was thought that enhanced human males had died out."

Mariana stood, her brain nicely mellow from the wine. "I need to think about all of this and get some sleep."

"In the morning, we're getting you out of here," Raine said, no give on his sharp face.

Mariana walked right at him and stopped an inch away. "Maybe. Unless I decide to mate you." She'd felt right with him from the beginning, and that had to mean something. So she lifted up on her tiptoes and kissed him.

Hard.

Chapter 14

Raine tossed and turned in the guest bed as the rain gentled outside, barely tapping against the window. He made plans for the next day and tried to decide the safest place for Mariana to relocate. The brand on his palm burned hotter than ever with her just in the next room. He'd told her everything, and she'd needed to sleep.

That was fine, but in the morning, she'd do as he said. While his time was limited, he'd find her safety before he left.

The door to the bedroom opened and outlined her sweet body.

He sat up and let the blankets fall to his waist. So much for protecting her. He hadn't even heard she was up, such was his preoccupation with her safety. "Mariana?" He listened to the world around them and could find no threats.

She audibly swallowed and walked on bare feet to the side of the bed. She wore a short nightie that appeared white in the soft light coming from the kitchen. Her nipples were hard beneath the silk. "Yes."

His heart started thundering. "What are you doing here?" He clenched the bedcovers to keep from reaching for her.

"I'm done thinking." She lifted the covers off him and then set a knee on the mattress before sliding her leg over to straddle his nude body. "You said you loved me."

"I do." His voice sounded desperate and his vocal cords ripped.

She placed her soft hands on his chest while her heated core was right on his aching cock. Only the very thin silky layer of her panties kept them apart. "I never believed in love at first sight until you. That first night you walked into the anger management group, I knew my life had changed. But I figured it was just me."

The marking on his palm cut deep, and he bit his lip to keep from growling. Her scent surrounded him, filling his head. His heart thumped hard, already seeking hers to find the familiar rhythm. "It wasn't just you."

"I trust you." She leaned over and kissed his neck.

He couldn't breathe. "You shouldn't."

Her lips wandered up to his jawline. "Why not?" she breathed.

He reached for her hair, tangled his fingers, and pulled her head back. The noise she made was not one of protest, and she pressed harder down on him. "I explained the danger you'd be in. Every day. Forever." He couldn't think with her soft body so close.

"You explained very well." She couldn't move her head, but she curled her fingernails into his pecs. "I'm in danger now. Staying human keeps me in danger, too. The danger I choose is with you."

Oh, God. It was more than he could've ever hoped. Once he'd told her the truth, he'd figured she'd do the smart and safe thing and stay away from him. "I can make you safe for your life."

"I want more than my life." Since he still held her head, she wiggled her soft butt against his thighs.

Fire lanced to his balls. He couldn't keep the groan quiet this time. The female was going to kill him. "Stop playing. We need to talk."

"Who's playing?" She ground down on him, and he was lost.

He clenched her hip and rolled them over, settling between her thighs and keeping his grip on her hair. He lifted up on one elbow so he didn't crush her. "Listen to me."

She arched against him, moaning as her nipples scraped along his chest, even through the silk. "I am listening."

"You're not." He tightened his hold until she had no choice but to meet his gaze. "If you think your movements will be curtailed because of the Kurjans, that's nothing compared to being my mate."

Her smile was sweet and unconcerned. "I trust you, Raine."

The words shot right to his heart and then kept going...somewhere much deeper. Somewhere only his mate could hit. But he owed her the full truth, even if he couldn't explain it very well. "I'm nearly four centuries old, sweetheart." The words rolled out of him while her heated core tempted him beyond what he thought he could refuse.

"I know." She cupped his jaw with one small hand.

"You don't know." Everything inside him wanted to take what she'd offered. But he'd vowed to himself to keep her safe, and that could include from him. "I'm not modern and never intend to be. If I mated, it wouldn't be a modern arrangement where we meet up every month. Even if that's what you eventually wanted."

"I love you, Raine." She blushed a light peach. "We've only known each other a few months, but I feel it. I know it. I don't want to have a business relationship with you. I want to build a life together."

It was more than he'd ever hoped to have. "I'm bossy."

"I know." She laughed.

He kissed her nose, unable to stop himself. "I'm possessive and protective."

"I've noticed that as well." She lifted her knees and managed to trap his hips between her soft thighs. "I can hold my own."

His grin felt primitive. "My word is law, baby. You agree to mate me, you agree that I mean that statement." It felt freeing to finally be himself.

Her smile held dare. "I understand that's what you think. Some laws were meant to be broken." She scratched along his jaw to tug on his earlobe, setting his body ablaze.

He'd never been able to turn away from a challenge, and this one he wanted to keep forever. "Tell me you get me," he whispered, this time grinding against her.

She gasped, and a flush covered her face. "I get you."

Oh, they would see about that. "I hope you know what you're getting into." He reached down and pulled the nightie over her head, revealing those peach-colored nipples that kept teasing him.

"Ditto," she moaned, grasping his shoulder. "I want this. Want you. All of you."

"You've got me." He leaned down and kissed her, way past the warning stage. They both wanted to go forward, and he loved her. He'd keep her safe, and she'd let him. For now, he moved down her body and ripped her tiny panties away.

One touch of his mouth and she went off, crying out his name. He let her ride out the waves. "Let's hear that again," he murmured against her, nipping at her clit.

* * * *

Mariana tugged on Raine's hair, trying to get him up her body. Three orgasms was enough. He growled against her core, and the low rumble carried through her entire body. She jerked and sighed, taking more of him.

He licked and nipped, bit and sucked. Somehow, his hands and mouth were everywhere. She felt herself driving up again and then fell over with barely a whimper, her body undulating with crashing waves stronger than her voice.

Finally, he let her rest as he kissed her thighs, her hipbones, her abs and then her breasts. Taking his time, killing her, he suckled each until her nipples were just aching nerves of need. Then he kissed her clavicle, her neck, and her cheeks. When he took her mouth again, it was with a lazy passion that turned wild way too fast.

How did he do that?

He held her in place, claiming everything with just his mouth. He commanded her response, and she gave it to him, her body too attuned to his to do anything else. His firm hand grasped her butt, and he pushed inside her, going slowly but taking no quarter.

Her body softened and stretched around him, slick after the multiple orgasms. Even so, she had to catch her breath at the exquisite pressure until he was balls deep inside her. It was more than she could've ever imagined.

He started moving then, in and out, setting up a rough rhythm she could only hold on and ride. Each scrape of nerves inside her had her quaking as she built up to yet another climax. He went faster and harder, partially lifting her off the bed, controlling them both. With the slightest twist of his hips, he hit her G-spot, and the entire room sheeted white as she climaxed. She arched against him and shut her eyes, taken over by the exquisite pleasure. "Raine," she sighed, coming down and going limp.

He kept pounding mercilessly, driving her up again. This time, her body was a jangle of nerves that all held breath. It was too much and yet, she needed more.

He pulled out and flipped her around, yanking her up on all fours. Then he shoved inside again and hit a spot that shot electricity through her limbs.

Grasping the back of her neck, he forced her head to the pillow and then wrapped an arm around her waist and lifted her against him. She turned her head to breathe and let him position her, crying out in pleasure when he angled over her clit somehow.

He was behind her, in control, and she'd never felt safer in her entire life.

One of his talented hands found her well-loved nipple and tweaked it with two fingers.

She jerked and then moaned as more need rushed to her core. It was so much. He hammered harder, pistoning inside her, laying claim in a way she would've never believed.

He released her waist and manacled his hands in her hair, tugging her head and forcing her to arch her back as he continued to pound inside her. "Tell me you're sure about this."

"I'm sure," she whispered, unable to say anything else. She wanted him. Forever.

A blinding pain sizzled into her hip just as he leaned over her and sliced his fangs into her neck. She catapulted into an orgasm so intense she could only close her eyes and sob his name. Over and over, there was only Raine Maxwell. Finally, her body released her from the whirlwind, and she went lax.

He ground against her and came, his body bucking violently. His fangs retracted, and he licked her wound clean before releasing her.

She flopped to the bed with her eyes already closing. Exhausted. "Raine."

"I'm here, sweetheart." He wrapped around her, settling the bedcovers over them. Then he gently kissed her head and smoothed her hair away from her face. "Are you all right?"

"Sleepy," she mumbled, already falling into dreamland. He spooned her from behind, and safety had never felt so good or warm. "Love you, Raine."

His breath caught against her back, and he held her tighter. "I love you, too. No matter what, Mariana. It's you and me forever." He caressed her arm to hold her hand, his big and broad around hers. "Trust me."

"I do," she said, meaning every word, trying to fight sleep. She should enjoy this moment. It was a big one. "Am I immortal yet?"

His chuckle stirred her hair. "No. That takes a little time. You are mated, though."

Yeah. Her hip felt like it was on fire. "You transferred the marking?"

"Yes. I'll still have one on my hand, but it'll be lighter and won't burn me so often." He kissed her head again. "Go to sleep."

He was already getting bossy with her. On that thought, she grinned and went to sleep.

Chapter 15

Mariana stretched herself awake against a hard male body. She was sore in all sorts of interesting places but had never felt more alive. "Do you still love me?" she murmured.

"More than ever." His lips were still against her head. "Want me to show you?"

She stretched again and then winced. "I might need a break."

He kissed her. "No break." Then he chuckled. His phone rang, and he stretched one long arm over her to take it from the bedside table.

Little tingles erupted where their skin touched. Maybe she didn't need a break.

"Maxwell," he answered. Then he sighed and stiffened. "No, Sheriff. You can talk to my attorney." He listened for a while. "Are you serious?"

Mariana turned over to face him and then definitely felt like she didn't need a break. A lock of dark hair had fallen on his forehead and sexy scruff covered his decidedly sculpted jaw. His eyes were a mellow moss green in the morning.

He rolled those eyes. "Fine." Then that jaw hardened. "Mariana is fine, thank you. She does not need to attend." He ended the call.

She indulged herself by running her palm along his whiskers. "What's going on?"

"The sheriff assures me that charges won't be filed but one of his deputies has a new lead on your stalker and somehow I'm involved so he wants to talk to me. He assures me I'm a victim and not a suspect." The dryness of Raine's voice made her chuckle.

"You're a victim? Ha." She leaned in to kiss his jaw.

"Right. I'm going to get this over with." He sat up and pressed the phone to his ear. "Hey, Cade. I mated Mariana last night. Could you get the word out to the Kurjans that they're too late? I think they're wrapped up enough with other fights that they'll let this one go. Yeah. Agreed. And there's no way they know about our real enemies, so I'm not worried about that. Yet." He ended the call.

Mariana sat up, and her mouth watered. The male had a very fine chest. "You just tell the Kurjans that kind of news?"

"Not usually." His grin was too sexy to be boyish this morning. "But they have a lot going on, so this is a loss they'll just have to suck up. I'm not worried about it, and Cade will get the message to them."

Well, that was one relief, at least. "When will you be back?" She could make a nice breakfast for them. While she should be feeling a little shy or overwhelmed, in truth, she felt fantastic. Like she should awaken next to Raine every morning. She grinned.

He grinned back. "I'm happy, too."

Now that was exactly what she'd wanted to hear. "I'll make breakfast while you're gone."

"Nope." He lifted the phone to his ear again and dialed. "Hey, Tabi. Can Mariana hang with you for about an hour while I go deal with the sheriff? Yeah? No problem. Thanks." He tossed the phone on the bed and moved for his duffle on the floor.

Mariana stood. "I don't need a babysitter. I'll be fine here." She twisted to see the marking on her hip. A perfect M with jagged lines. It looked like an intricate tattoo. "Wow."

His eyes flared. "That's beautiful."

It really was. She rocked back on her heels and stretched. "I like it."

"Good thing." He yanked on jeans and reached for a shirt.

"I'm staying here, Raine." She looked around for her nightie but didn't see it. Oh well. She should get dressed anyway.

"No." He put on the shirt and padded toward the bathroom. "You're not immortal yet, and I want the demoness around just in case. We still don't know who was stalking you."

Mariana put her hands on her hips. "Is this what you meant about your word being law?"

"It's a start." He disappeared into the bathroom.

Well, they were not going to continue in this vein, but for now, she didn't mind talking to Tabi about this whole immortality situation. So she hurried to dress. After brushing her teeth and putting her hair in a ponytail, she put on a minimum of makeup and met Raine in the living room. "I hope you know I'm going along with this because I want to see Tabi."

"Okay." Raine took her out to a new blue truck in the driveway.

She stumbled, and he righted her by the arm. "Where did this come from?"

"I ordered it," he said, assisting her up into the passenger seat. "We're very comfortable. I'll make the accounts joint when I get the chance."

She held out a hand. "I don't need your money, Raine."

"It's our money." He shut the door before she could argue.

She rolled her eyes. The truck was pretty nice. They made the drive in the soft sunshine, with the rain having finally stopped.

After buying three lattes, Raine drove her to Tabi's house and handed over the drinks. "Stay here until I pick you up." He kissed her on the chin, both cheeks, and then her forehead, making her go all gushy inside. Then he waited until she'd reached the door to Evan's comfortable home before driving off.

Tabi opened the door and reached for the lattes. "Awesome. Thank you."

"Sure." Mariana kept a drink and walked inside, expecting to see Evan. Instead, a pretty blonde with a black eye sat on the sofa and accepted the coffee from Tabi.

Tabi smiled. "Mariana, this is Louise Baker. She's currently getting divorced from Deputy Johnny Baker, the sheriff's kid, and is going to need a good shrink."

Louise sipped her latte. "It's nice to meet you."

"You, too." Mariana took a seat. "Raine and I are figuring out what to do, but I'd like to open an office here in town. You'd be my first client." She remembered hearing that Johnny was an ass who liked to hit. It was good this girl had left him, and Mariana could help her. She wanted to help.

Louise blanched. "I, um, can't pay you much."

Mariana waved a hand. "No worries. In fact, if I open an office, I'll need a receptionist and office manager. What do you say?"

Tabi beamed behind her latte cup.

Louise frowned and then steeled her shoulders. "I'd love to help."

"Perfect," Tabi said, nearly hopping in place with her blonde hair flying. "I love it when a plan comes together." She sniffed the air and then zeroed in on Mariana. "Don't you? Yep. A good plan. Yay."

Mariana hid a smile. Obviously Tabi knew that Raine and she had mated. "I have questions for you later," she said.

"I'm sure," Tabi said, grinning widely.

Louise's phone rang, and she pulled it out of a brightly patched purse. "Hello?" She paled. "I know, but...okay. Yes." She replaced the phone in her bag, and her hand trembled.

Mariana reached for her hand. "What's wrong?"

The girl swallowed. She had to be only around eighteen. "That was Johnny. Today was the last day we have our rental house, and he's moving everything. He said if I don't come get the rest of my things, he'll take them to the dump. I wouldn't care, but my grandma left me her Belleek china from Ireland."

Tabi grabbed her keys off the sofa table. "Let's go get your stuff. It's okay. Johnny's afraid of me after I beat him up last year and ended up in anger management classes." She laughed. "The idiot attacked me along with a couple of his buddies. He won't dare do it again." Then she frowned. "Unfortunately. To be honest, I'd really like to kick him again."

Louise faltered and then nodded. "Yes. Okay. I'm tired of being afraid of him. Let's go."

Mariana stood.

Tabi waved her back down. "Not you, sister. You're supposed to stay here and under the radar until Raine gets back. I promised in exchange for the lattes. You take it easy and watch some television or something."

Mariana sighed. "Where's Evan?"

"He had a campaign breakfast," Tabi said. "He should be home in an hour or so. Louise and I will be back probably before he returns. I'll lock the door. Bye, Mariana."

Maybe all immortals were bossy. Mariana watched the women go and then looked around. Well, she could watch some television. Two dogs played out back, and she could go throw sticks for them. Or she could take a little nap on the sofa.

She was a bit tired. Maybe it was the whole increase in chromosomal pairs or something.

A knock sounded on the door before she could make up her mind. "What did you forget?" She laughed and opened the door to see Sheriff Baker on the porch. "Sheriff." Was he looking for his daughter-in-law? Well, his soon to be ex-daughter-in-law.

"Hi. There was a problem at the station, and Maxwell sent me to get you." The sheriff's buzz cut was sharper than ever and his uniform was creased mercilessly. "You can bring your coffee."

Mariana frowned. "What kind of problem?"

The sheriff rubbed his clean-shaven chin. "He got into an altercation with two deputies, and the only thing that would calm the guy down was my promising to come get you."

Her instincts flared wide awake but she kept calm. "Oh." She nodded. "All right." There was no way on God's green earth that Raine would ever want the sheriff to fetch her. "Let me grab my purse." She moved to slam and lock the door, but he put one foot in the way. She kicked his foot and tried again, but he shoved the door open, and she flew back into the sofa table. The edge caught her ribcage, and pain shot through her. She winced.

He pointed his gun at her. "That was so unnecessary. Get into the car before I cuff you. Now."

"No." She turned to run, and he caught her by the arm, pressing it up beneath her shoulder blade with enough pressure to draw tears to her eyes.

"Move." He pushed her onto the porch and slammed the door, forcing her to his police car, where he put her in the backseat and shut the door.

She stretched her arm out, wincing as the tendons protested. "What the hell are you doing?"

He moved into the driver's seat and started the car, driving away from the house. "I just wanted to talk to you. Is that so bad? Why do you have to make everything so damn difficult?"

"I'm sorry," she said, not meaning it. How could she get out of this? Had he arrested her? If so, for what?

"You're in danger, and I want to help you. It's my job, and I'm tired of everyone fighting me on it."

She winced. The guy sucked at his job, and he was right that nobody cooperated.

He stared at her through the rearview mirror. "When you received those three dozen white roses, I knew I could help you. That I could protect you. Why won't you let me?"

She opened her mouth to appease him and then paused. "Three dozen? I didn't tell you there were three dozen. I just told you that I'd received white roses." Most people would assume it was a dozen, right? Her brain reeled. Wait a minute.

He parked beneath a tree in a vacant parking lot next to an abandoned fast food joint. "I really wish you wouldn't have figured that out."

Her chin dropped. "You sent me the roses?" How was that possible?

"I care for you. A lot. I know I'm married, but you're special. You and I could have something really great together, if you'd just give me a chance." He partially turned to face her, and the divider between the seats was open.

She tried to filter facts into place. "Did you send me flowers in Dallas?"

"No," he burst out. "Of course not. However, when I first saw you, I did a background check and discovered your case in Dallas. So I sent you flowers here—"

"Thinking I'd turn to you for protection?" she asked.

He nodded, his nostrils flaring. "But you turned to that Maxwell asshole instead."

Raine. Oh, God. The sheriff had called him earlier that morning. "Where is Raine?"

"He's at the station answering questions with a couple of deputies." The sheriff waved away the question. "I just needed time to talk to you."

Wait a minute. She had a stalker in Dallas, was followed by Raine, kidnapped by Kurjans, and now taken by the sheriff? She barked out a hysterical laugh. This was crazy. "I must have some seriously whacked out pheromones," she muttered.

"What?" the sheriff asked.

She eyed the side doors. They were locked, and there was no way out. Well, there was one way. She bunched her legs and burst through the opening in the divider between the front and rear seats, landing on her knees and hitting her chin on the dash. She moved to the right and kicked back with one leg, smashing Baker's nose.

He howled and reached for his gun. She pivoted to grab it.

His door was jerked open, and he flew out to land on his ass.

Raine leaned in. "You okay?"

She gulped and nodded.

Raine turned and punched Sheriff Baker in the jaw. The sheriff fell back into the mud, arms splayed, out cold. "Damn it," Raine muttered.

Mariana scrambled out of the vehicle. "You only got to hit him once."

Raine turned on her. "This is what happens when you don't stay where I tell you to stay."

"Wasn't my fault," she said quietly. "How are you here?"

He pulled her close and kissed her. Hard and then soft. "I figured out it was a scam after the first question, and I headed right for you. Caught your scent."

Her eyebrows rose. "Literally?"

"Yeah." He kissed her again and held her close. "I love you, Mariana Lopez."

She snuggled into his hard body. "I love you, too. Forever."

He chuckled. "It's going to be an adventure."

"I hope so." Then she laughed along with him.

Epilogue

The boisterous crowd had bundled up against the early snow, their happiness obvious as they enjoyed the outdoor festivities following Evan O'Connell being made sheriff. He'd won easily, and Sheriff Baker had conceded…from a jail cell. The guy would face some time for kidnapping Mariana and blowing up the truck. Raine was glad about that.

Kind of. He would've liked to have gotten in a couple more punches.

Mariana hustled up with apple ciders in both mitten-covered hands. With a white knit hat on her hair, she looked adorable. A snowflake landed on her nose. "Here. It's delicious."

"Thanks." He'd watched her the entire time she'd worked the crowd with Tabi and was comfortable that she was safe. The drink was good. Nice and warm.

Her phone rang, and she pulled it out of her pocket to glance at the face. "It's Laura." She quickly pressed a button. "Hi. You're on speaker with Raine. He can't wait to meet you when you visit next month."

Raine smiled even as he scanned the gathering for any threats. "Hi.'"

"Hi. Can't wait to meet you, too." Laura sounded distracted. "You're not going to believe this, but we've found your stalker. Do you remember a computer tech named Kenny Jilloby?"

She swallowed. "Kind of? I think he worked on our system a couple of times."

"Yes, he did. We just caught him sending roses to another woman from the same building, and he admitted to sending you flowers and notes. Didn't once try to follow you. The guy has issues, though."

Raine made a mental note to have Cade find out everything there was about good ole Kenny.

Mariana smiled. "Great job finding him."

"Thanks. The other news is that he has no clue where you went, so he switched to another great love, as he called her. Leaving was a good move. He's in custody now, so that's over." Laura shuffled papers. "Oh. Gotta go. See you two soon." The line went dead.

Mariana tucked the phone away,. "You're going to love her."

Sure. If Mariana loved her, he'd protect her as well. "I'm sure."

Tabi bounced up with Evan behind her. "I'm so glad this happened. A new sheriff." She motioned Abby and Noah over. The lovebirds had been back a week and had definitely pitched in to help. "I have awesome news. We have the corrupt sheriff out of office, and Abby is going to run for mayor next year. I'm running her campaign."

Abby stumbled. "Mayor? I'm not running for mayor."

Her mate, vampire Noah Siosal, sighed. "I have a feeling you are. Right, demoness?"

Tabi grinned. "Yep. You turned in all the necessary documents weeks ago. I mean, the mayor, sheriff, and that judge railroaded you when your dirtbag ex set you up. Don't you want to stick it to them?"

Abby smoothed her dark hair away from her face. "Not really. I'm happy." She smiled at her mate.

Tabi sighed. "Fine. Then don't you want to help clean up the town? Make it safe and good again?"

Good plug.

Abby slowly nodded.

"Good," Tabi said. "Evan and Noah will be honest police officers, and you'll be a great mayor. Mariana and I are contributing to the town with our businesses, and once you're mayor, you can appoint Raine as a judge when that dirty one faces a scandal."

Raine and Abby jumped as one. "What scandal?" Abby asked.

Tabi shrugged. "He's been skimming the books on a nonprofit he started with his brother. We'll time the disclosure just right."

Evan tugged his demoness closer. "Tell me you didn't create this situation."

"I'd never do that," the blonde protested. Then she paused. "Okay. I'd do that, but I didn't this time. He's really skimming."

Raine gave in to temptation and drew his mate closer to his side. "I don't want to be a judge and have plenty to do with my investments and businesses."

Tabi shrugged. "Come on. It's just for a couple of decades. We all set out to clean up this town, and that's the last step. I think it's a great idea. I'm sure that Mariana would be so proud of you if you'd be a judge. Surely you've learned some law in your centuries on earth."

Truth be told, he'd gone to a couple of law schools. He looked at Mariana.

She snuggled into his side. "It's your call. I love you regardless."

He sighed. "Fine, but just for a couple of decades. Then you find somebody else." He grasped Mariana's hand. "We'll be back." They strode away as the snow fell lightly around them.

"She has your number," Mariana said as he lifted her to sit on top of a wooden picnic table.

He shrugged. "I can be a judge for a while if it cleans up the town. Do you like your practice here?"

She nodded. "I do. For a couple of decades." Her smile was sweet and calmed everything inside him. "So long as we're together, I'll go anywhere."

He leaned over and kissed her, overwhelmed that this brilliant, kind, and talented female wanted to be with him. No matter what. Their lives would be full of adventure, some drama, and lots of love. Even if the Maxwell enemies found them, they'd triumph. They'd deal with it all together. "I'm glad I made you mine, mate."

She grinned, and her eyes sparkled. "Me too, Vampire."

* * * *

Also from 1001 Dark Nights and Rebecca Zanetti, discover Vixen, Vengeance, Blaze Erupting, Tangled, Teased, and Tricked.

Sign up for the 1001 Dark Nights Newsletter
and be entered to win a Tiffany Key necklace.

There's a contest every month!

Go to www.1001DarkNights.com to subscribe

As a bonus, all subscribers can download
FIVE FREE exclusive books!

Discover 1001 Dark Nights Collection Eight

For more information, visit www.1001DarkNights.com.

DRAGON REVEALED by Donna Grant
A Dragon Kings Novella

CAPTURED IN INK by Carrie Ann Ryan
A Montgomery Ink: Boulder Novella

SECURING JANE by Susan Stoker
A SEAL of Protection: Legacy Series Novella

WILD WIND by Kristen Ashley
A Chaos Novella

DARE TO TEASE by Carly Phillips
A Dare Nation Novella

VAMPIRE by Rebecca Zanetti
A Dark Protectors/Rebels Novella

MAFIA KING by Rachel Van Dyken
A Mafia Royals Novella

THE GRAVEDIGGER'S SON by Darynda Jones
A Charley Davidson Novella

FINALE by Skye Warren
A North Security Novella

MEMORIES OF YOU by J. Kenner
A Stark Securities Novella

SLAYED BY DARKNESS by Alexandra Ivy
A Guardians of Eternity Novella

TREASURED by Lexi Blake
A Masters and Mercenaries Novella

THE DAREDEVIL by Dylan Allen
A Rivers Wilde Novella

BOND OF DESTINY by Larissa Ione
A Demonica Novella

THE CLOSE-UP by Kennedy Ryan
A Hollywood Renaissance Novella

MORE THAN POSSESS YOU by Shayla Black
A More Than Words Novella

HAUNTED HOUSE by Heather Graham
A Krewe of Hunters Novella

MAN FOR ME by Laurelin Paige
A Man In Charge Novella

THE RHYTHM METHOD by Kylie Scott
A Stage Dive Novella

JONAH BENNETT by Tijan
A Bennett Mafia Novella

CHANGE WITH ME by Kristen Proby
A With Me In Seattle Novella

THE DARKEST DESTINY by Gena Showalter
A Lords of the Underworld Novella

Also from Blue Box Press

THE LAST TIARA by M.J. Rose

THE CROWN OF GILDED BONES by Jennifer L. Armentrout
A Blood and Ash Novel

THE MISSING SISTER by Lucinda Riley

Discover More Rebecca Zanetti

Vixen
A Dark Protectors/Rebels Novella

Tabi Rusko has a simple to-do list: Rob a bank, steal a recording, set up a lucrative factory, and survive the assassins on her tail. Sure, she's a demoness with the cunning and instincts that come with her species, but she's always spent more time exploring than training, and her fighting skills are okay at best. One sexy man, a human cop no less, is responsible for her being stuck in a small hick town and forced into a human anger-management group that's crazier than her. To make matters worse, his dangerous blue eyes and hard body leave her breathless and ready to rumble, and his overbearing attitude is a challenge a demoness can't refuse.

Evan O'Connell just wants to enjoy his time out of the military by policing a small town and hopefully pulling cats from trees and helping old ladies cross the street before he succumbs to the disease plaguing him. The last thing he needs is a stunning, too sexy, pain in the butt blonde casing his bank and causing a ruckus everywhere she goes. There's something different about her that he can't figure out, and when she offers him immortality in exchange for her freedom, he discovers that isn't enough. One touch of her, a whirlwind beyond his imagination, and he wants the Vixen to be his forever, as soon as he takes care of the centuries old killers on her tail.

* * * *

Vengeance
A Dark Protectors/Rebels Novella

Vengeance and revenge are the only forces driving vampire soldier Noah Siosal since losing his brother to an enemy he's been unable to find. He's searched every corner of the globe, going through adversaries and piling up bodies until finally getting a lead. The last place he wants to be is in a ridiculous anger management group with people expressing feelings instead of taking action. Until one fragile human, a green-eyed sweetheart being stalked by danger, catches his eye. One touch, and he realizes vengeance can't be anywhere near her.

Anger and self-preservation are the only motivations Abby Miller needs or wants right now. Falsely accused of attacking the man who's terrorized her for years, she's forced as a plea bargain to attend an anger management counseling group with people with some serious rage issues, while learning true self defense on the side. Yet a man, one more primal than any she's ever met, draws her in a way and into a world deadlier than she's ever imagined. He offers her protection, but she finds the fight is really for his heart, and she's ready to battle.

* * * *

Blaze Erupting
Scorpius Syndrome/A Brigade Novella

Hugh Johnson is nobody's hero, and the idea of being in the limelight makes him want to growl. He takes care of his brothers, does his job, and enjoys a mellow evening hanging with his hound dog and watching the sports channel. So when sweet and sexy Ellie Smithers from his college chemistry class asks him to save millions of people from a nuclear meltdown, he doggedly steps forward while telling himself that the world hasn't changed and he can go back to his relaxing life. One look at Ellie and excitement doesn't seem so bad.

Eleanor Smithers knows that the Scorpius bacteria has and will change life as we know it, but that's a concern for another day. She's been hand-picked as the computer guru for The Brigade, which is the USA's first line of defense against all things Scorpius, including homegrown terrorists who've just been waiting for a chance to strike. Their target is a nuclear power plant in the east, and the only person who can help her is Hugh, the sexy, laconic, dangerous man she had a crush on so long ago.

* * * *

Tangled
A Dark Protectors—Reece Family Novella

Now that her mask has finally slipped…
Ginny O'Toole has spent a lifetime repaying her family's debt, and

she's finally at the end of her servitude with one last job. Of course, it couldn't be easy. After stealing the computer files that will free her once and for all, she finds herself on the run from a pissed off vampire who has never fallen for her helpless act. A deadly predator too sexy for his own good. If he doesn't knock it off, he's going to see just how powerful she can really be.

He won't be satisfied until she's completely bare.

Theo Reese had been more than irritated at the beautiful yet helpless witch he'd known a century ago, thinking she was just useless fluff who enjoyed messing with men's heads. The second he discovers she's a ruthless thief determined to bring down his family, his blood burns and his interest peaks, sending his true nature into hunting mode. When he finds her, and he will, she'll understand the real meaning of helpless.

* * * *

Tricked
A Dark Protectors—Reese Family Novella

He Might Save Her

Former police psychologist Ronni Alexander had it all before a poison attacked her heart and gave her a death sentence. Now, on her last leg, she has an opportunity to live if she mates a vampire. A real vampire. One night of sex and a good bite, and she'd live forever with no more weaknesses. Well, except for the vampire whose dominance is over the top, and who has no clue how to deal with a modern woman who can take care of herself.

She Might Kill Him

Jared Reese, who has no intention of ever mating for anything other than convenience, agrees to help out his new sister in law by saving her friend's life with a quick tussle in bed. The plan seems so simple. They'd mate, and he move on with his life and take risks as a modern pirate should. Except after one night with Ronni, one moment of her sighing his name, and he wants more than a mating of convenience. Now all he has to do is convince Ronni she wants the same thing. Good thing he's up for a good battle.

* * * *

Teased
A Dark Protectors—Reece Family Novella

The Hunter

For almost a century, the Realm's most deadly assassin, Chalton Reese, has left war and death in the past, turning instead to strategy, reason, and technology. His fingers, still stained with blood, now protect with a keyboard instead of a weapon. Until the vampire king sends him on one more mission; to hunt down a human female with the knowledge to destroy the Realm. A woman with eyes like emeralds, a brain to match his own, and a passion that might destroy them both—if the enemy on their heels doesn't do so first.

The Hunted

Olivia Roberts has foregone relationships with wimpy metro-sexuals in favor of pursuing a good story, bound and determined to uncover the truth, any truth. When her instincts start humming about missing proprietary information, she has no idea her search for a story will lead her to a ripped, sexy, and dangerous male beyond any human man. Setting aside the unbelievable fact that he's a vampire and she's his prey, she discovers that trusting him is the only chance they have to survive the danger stalking them both.

Rebel's Karma

Dark Protectors, Book 13
By Rebecca Zanetti
Coming June 8, 2021

There's no denying destiny...

For too long, Benjamin Reese has masked his deadly skills and temper with loyalty and humor. A vampire-demon hybrid, he fiercely protects his family, guards his brothers, and destroys the enemy without mercy. But when he discovers one fragile, beautiful blonde—a woman once mated to a Kurjan, no less—every primal instinct he has buried for centuries roars to life. With the mating mark she roused on his hand entwining their fates, no one will prevent him from keeping her safe and making her his, forever...

Or desire...

Karma wishes she could remember her last name. Or if she even had one. All she has in this confusing new world is a desperate duty to save the innocent. That means destroying the dark, dangerous, and desirable Benjamin Reese and everything he loves—an impossible task even before his touch arouses a passionate hunger she can't afford. She's certain a deadly enemy watches her every move, but it's not until Benny kisses her that she tastes true danger...

* * * *

An excerpt from Rebel's Karma (Benny's Story)

Karma had bigger things to worry about than the life of this massive hybrid. She allowed herself one moment to stare into his unusual eyes. Oh, many immortals had metallic-silver eyes, gold eyes, even copper or purple. But his were a combination of all argent colors, mingling into a hard-edged glint, even with the humor lurking there. In another time, she might've thought him beautiful. She'd learned long ago that beauty could mask the darkest of evils.

Vampires were bad, demons were bad, and this male was a hybrid of both. When he decided to kill her—and he would at some point—she wouldn't stand much chance of surviving. Yet she still couldn't comprehend why he'd come for her. "Why are you here?"

"For you. To rescue you because I couldn't last time." He stretched out his arms and healed a broken finger in his left hand.

His words didn't make any sense. "Why?" Surely his ego wasn't such that he'd risked his life just because she'd rejected his help last time. She wasn't worth that.

He sighed. "I'd hoped to ease you into the truth, but here it is." He held up his right hand, showing a demon marking with a jagged *R* in the center. The *R* was a crest representing his surname: Reese. Demons mated with a branding and a bite—the marking was transferred from the demon to the mate during sex.

Her mouth dropped open, and she hurried to shut it. "You're mated?" Why did that thought nauseate her? How odd.

"No. The brand appeared when I touched you three years ago." His chin lowered, and he studied her, towering over her even as he sat. "When you shoved me away and refused to get into that helicopter with me." He didn't sound happy.

She snorted and then quickly recovered. "Impossible. I'm already mated." Well, she had been mated a couple of centuries ago, although her Kurjan mate had died shortly thereafter. Sometimes she forgot what he had looked like, and that was fine with her. "Your brand must have appeared for someone else."

"No." Benjamin looked down at the dark marking. "The mark hasn't faded a bit, and it's pulsing like a live wire now that you're near."

Oh, Lord. Her research on Benjamin suggested he might be insane. Dangerous and unstable? There was no way she could succeed in this mission. "Benjamin—"

"Benny. Might as well get cozy with me now." His smile held charm and determination that warmed her in an unexpected way.

For the second time in her life, she let her instincts take over. "Just leave. Take an opening and find freedom," she whispered tersely, her stomach cramping. "Forget about me."

"Not a chance." His gaze ran over her face like a physical touch.

Movement sounded down the tunnel, and she stiffened.

Benjamin tensed and set his jaw. "Get ready, darlin'. We're about to escape this place."

About Rebecca Zanetti

New York Times and *USA Today bestselling* author Rebecca Zanetti has published more than fifty novels, which have been translated into several languages, with millions of copies sold world-wide. Her books have received Publisher's Weekly starred reviews, won RT Reviewer Choice awards, and have been featured in Entertainment Weekly, Woman's World, and Women's Day Magazines. Her novels have also been included in Amazon best books of the year and have been favorably reviewed in both the Washington Post and the New York Times Book Reviews. Rebecca has ridden in a locked Chevy trunk, has asked the unfortunate delivery guy to release her from a set of handcuffs, and has discovered the best silver mine shafts in which to bury a body...all in the name of research. Honest. Find Rebecca at: www.RebeccaZanetti.com

Discover 1001 Dark Nights

ABANDON by Rachel Van Dyken ~ THE OPEN DOOR by Laurelin Paige~ CLOSER by Kylie Scott ~ SOMETHING JUST LIKE THIS by Jennifer Probst ~ BLOOD NIGHT by Heather Graham ~ TWIST OF FATE by Jill Shalvis ~ MORE THAN PLEASURE YOU by Shayla Black ~ WONDER WITH ME by Kristen Proby ~ THE DARKEST ASSASSIN by Gena Showalter

COLLECTION SEVEN
THE BISHOP by Skye Warren ~ TAKEN WITH YOU by Carrie Ann Ryan ~ DRAGON LOST by Donna Grant ~ SEXY LOVE by Carly Phillips ~ PROVOKE by Rachel Van Dyken ~ RAFE by Sawyer Bennett ~ THE NAUGHTY PRINCESS by Claire Contreras ~ THE GRAVEYARD SHIFT by Darynda Jones ~ CHARMED by Lexi Blake ~ SACRIFICE OF DARKNESS by Alexandra Ivy ~ THE QUEEN by Jen Armentrout ~ BEGIN AGAIN by Jennifer Probst ~ VIXEN by Rebecca Zanetti ~ SLASH by Laurelin Paige ~ THE DEAD HEAT OF SUMMER by Heather Graham ~ WILD FIRE by Kristen Ashley ~ MORE THAN PROTECT YOU by Shayla Black ~ LOVE SONG by Kylie Scott ~ CHERISH ME by J. Kenner ~ SHINE WITH ME by Kristen Proby

Discover Blue Box Press
TAME ME by J. Kenner ~ TEMPT ME by J. Kenner ~ DAMIEN by J. Kenner ~ TEASE ME by J. Kenner ~ REAPER by Larissa Ione ~ THE SURRENDER GATE by Christopher Rice ~ SERVICING THE TARGET by Cherise Sinclair ~ THE LAKE OF LEARNING by Steve Berry and MJ Rose ~ THE MUSEUM OF MYSTERIES by Steve Berry and MJ Rose ~ TEASE ME by J. Kenner ~ FROM BLOOD AND ASH by Jennifer L. Armentrout ~ QUEEN MOVE by Kennedy Ryan ~ THE HOUSE OF LONG AGO by Steve Berry and MJ Rose ~ THE BUTTERFLY ROOM by Lucinda Riley ~ A KINGDOM OF FLESH AND FIRE by Jennifer L. Armentrout

On behalf of 1001 Dark Nights,

Liz Berry, M.J. Rose, and Jillian Stein would like to thank ~

Steve Berry
Doug Scofield
Benjamin Stein
Kim Guidroz
Social Butterfly PR
Ashley Wells
Asha Hossain
Chris Graham
Chelle Olson
Kasi Alexander
Jessica Johns
Dylan Stockton
Richard Blake
and Simon Lipskar

Made in the USA
Las Vegas, NV
12 April 2021